T0197339

QUESTION EVERYTHING

S. J. Riccobono

Order this book online at www.trafford.com
or email orders@trafford.com

Most Trafford titles are also available at major online book retailers.

© Copyright 2011 S. J. Riccobono.
All rights reserved. No part of this publication may be reproduced, stored in a
retrieval system, or transmitted, in any form or by any means, electronic, mechanical,
photocopying, recording, or otherwise, without the written prior permission of the author.

Printed in the United States of America.

ISBN: 978-1-4669-0917-5 (sc)
ISBN: 978-1-4669-0918-2 (e)

Library of Congress Control Number: 2011963031

Trafford rev. 12/20/2011

 www.trafford.com

North America & international
toll-free: 1 888 232 4444 (USA & Canada)
phone: 250 383 6864 ♦ fax: 812 355 4082

To my parents, John and Dorothy.

CONTENTS

EXPEDITION

Ralston Max was one hell of a hunter. Considered young for his expertise, he and Marigold Dancer were hired by a legendary trapper and business entrepreneur to gather some of the most exotic animals from the furthest regions of space. Eager to showcase its recently constructed super zoo, United Earth paid a high price to assemble such a remarkable team.

Ralston slid his hand along the vibrating bulkheads of the science vessel on his way to the cargo hold where the animals were kept on three levels surrounding an open atrium. He joined Marigold and mission leader Jason Trumbel next to a high security cell where a sedated rock crag rested undisturbed behind thick windows. Ralston gazed at the brownish, gray armored creature with a seven foot circumference and ten muscular legs protruding symmetrically from its abdomen. "That was a close call, Jason. We almost lost her."

White haired Trumbel was dismissive. "But we didn't."

Marigold, at least ten years older than Ralston, brushed her thick wavy hair away from her face. "All that matters is no one was harmed."

Ralston was tentative. "This was a female. We're not going to be able to trap the larger male using your methods. We can't just arbitrarily stun it from a long distance. We need a precise, low intensity beam at close range."

"I tend to agree. By the time we trapped, sedated and beamed this female up, we almost lost her. Not to mention any self-inflicted damage that might have occurred inside the cage."

Marigold became defensive. "Jason, its standard procedure."

He scratched his head. "You're right. That's why we're doing it Ralston's way the next time."

Irritated, she pointed at her younger colleague. "His methods may be direct, but they put everyone at risk."

"Perhaps. But a male rock crag has never been successful trapped before, let alone kept alive in captivity."

"Don't worry, Jason. I'll get your crag up here in one piece."

Trumbel turned to Marigold. "You on board?"

She chuckled. "What can I say? You're the boss."

Jason remained on the science vessel as Ralston, Marigold, five veterinarians and their support staff transported to the drier southern region where narrow valleys split rocky cliffs. The atmosphere was similar to Earth and the sparse plant life rarely exceeded four feet in height. Ralston and his team gathered near the opening of a dry river bed between two imposing bluffs. A mild warm breeze swirled around their feet as Marigold scanned the quiet terrain.

"It's still there."

Ralston unfastened his equipment and dropped it to the ground. "This is prime crag territory. Animal trails and a clear overview."

"It's definitely waiting for a meal."

"The perfect predator. Nasty, relentless, yet cautious."

Marigold turned to the lead veterinarian. "Is your team ready?"

"I believe so."

Ralston gestured for them to close ranks. "Here's how it's going down. I'll walk ahead fifty feet, the vets will flank me. Marigold, I'll need that dead aim of yours to blast this thing if it panics and attacks."

"What about you? This thing is so fast, you wouldn't know what hit you."

He grinned at her, and then turned to the others. "I know the risks. I'm putting my ass on the line, so let's get it right." He glanced over at Marigold. "Just remember, do your job. You're my babysitter."

Ralston proceeded through the river bed with his laser pistol secured in its holster. His boots crunched the gravely sand; an invitation for any hungry rock crag. Up ahead, the creature's round mass lay vertically attached to the steep facade.

The support team kept their distance from Ralston and pressed up against the opposite side of the cliff. Other than his exaggerated footsteps, there was silence. Alerted to the intrusion, the creature released its grip and crept down the side of the rock face. Ralston was unaware of its movements, but Marigold followed its every step with her sensors. He glanced anxiously from side to side, knowing full well that up ahead was the ideal ambush spot.

The rock crag leapt with a sudden burst and propelled down the cliff face in seconds. It then gyrated and scurried horizontally across a lower shelf and aligned itself next to a ridge and waited for Ralston to pass underneath.

Understanding the cautious nature of the beast, Ralston was tempted to look up as a matter of self preservation, but knew he had to depend on the tenacity of the others. Any sudden move could spook the crag, who had settled down quietly with an unobstructed view of its prey. Moments later he walked under the crag and it sprung forcefully from its perch. About to pounce on him, the team directed an energy field that held it suspended in place just above his head. The crag's legs frantically stabbed at the air as the veterinarians ran under its stomach, administered a healthy dose of tranquilizers and rendered it unconscious. It was then transported safely to the science vessel and deposited in a cell next to the smaller female.

Ralston was breathing heavily. "That was awesome. I'd be lying if I said I wasn't scared shitless."

Marigold smirked. "A few more feet, and it would have been munching on a prime chunk of your head."

"Yeah? Maybe so. But it's ours now."

They returned to the ship and met up with Jason, who was admiring his new acquisition. "Beautiful, isn't it?"

"If you can call that ill tempered beast beautiful."

"Marigold, we have a breeding pair of rock crags. Nobody else can make that claim."

"True. But we only discovered them two years ago."

His impatience showed. "None the less, we're the first to bring them home." He patted Ralston on the shoulder. "Good job."

"Don't mention it."

An hour later, Jason ordered the science vessel on a three day's journey at high warp. During the down time, Ralston spotted Marigold in the galley and brought his tray of food over to her table. "Mind if I join you?"

She sipped her coffee. "Be my guest."

Distracted and hesitant, he looked out the window at the streaking stars. "So, what's your husband up to?"

"I rarely anticipate Jason's actions."

"Come on, Marigold. You must find it odd that we're traveling so far to retrieve a fairly accessible species. Gormalian Fire Moles are crowd pleasers, but they're certainly not rare."

"He must have his reasons."

Jason entered the galley robustly. "Well, if it isn't my two best trappers."

"What's this all about", Ralston asked? We're not hunting for moles, are we?

"Yes, I'm a little curious myself."

He laughed. "My own wife questioning me. All right. We're hunting for the Tabar Caluso."

Marigold was almost indignant. "It's one of the rarest species known. We don't even know where to find them."

He sat down and talked quietly. "What if I told you I met a trader that gave me pretty convincing evidence where we could find it?"

Ralston slowly nodded. "Judging by our flight path, we're heading right for the Noma Six quadrant."

Marigold tightened her fist. "That space is between us and the enemy. Are you mad?"

"The Drio Empire has no claim on Noma Six."

"Maybe not, Jason. But the Captain of our battleship escort won't see it that way."

He stood up and glared at them seriously. "I'm willing to take the gamble. Noma Six may be uncharted territory, but I've got clout with our government. They're really invested in our success."

Marigold submissively implored him. "Even if we find such an animal, if we don't return to Earth in a few weeks, our entire cargo may be at risk."

"You let me worry about that." He walked away unfazed.

Ralston picked up his utensils. "Some husband, you got."

Jason Trumbel was right about one thing. United Earth had considered this journey important enough to grant his request to penetrate the Noma Six quadrant. Although weary of such an endeavor, the Ellington's Captain followed orders and prepared for departure. Short of a Drio attack convoy, his vessel's massive firepower was more than capable of defending the smaller science vessel.

Jason received a final briefing by the Ellington Captain. "We've already notified the Drio Empire of our intentions."

"I didn't think it was any of their business. It's unclaimed space."

"Mr. Trumbel, they had no qualms about us entering Noma Six. But keep in mind that the Drio and United Earth have had difficulties with regional disputes. Both sides agreed to notify the other when or if entering an unclaimed quadrant."

"Fine. You notified, they agreed."

"If you don't mind me asking, these coordinates are fairly broad. How can you be certain of the planet's location?"

"It's an adventure, Captain. What you're really asking me, how can I trust the trader that relayed them to me? I don't have a good answer for that. But it wasn't a bad deal. I paid him one third up front, the rest upon capture. I'm sure that if you considered this little side trip too dangerous, we wouldn't be going."

"That is correct. We can fully protect your science vessel. We should be arriving in a few hours. You'll join me on the Bridge at that time?"

"You can count on it."

Three hours later they reduced to sub-light speed and headed for a nearby binary star system. Jason sat in a chair behind the Captain, who ordered his crew to scan the four giant gaseous planets. "Here we are, Mr. Trumbel, and it appears your planet does not exist."

"Any other star systems in this area."

The navigator turned around. "Another system three light years away."

"It's your call, Trumbel."

"By all means."

After a short jump, they arrived in a single star system with twenty planets. Most were completely barren, but one had a toxic atmosphere with pink stained vegetation; ideal for the Tabar Caluso. The helmsman maneuvered the Ellington into orbit and the science vessel followed. Jason transported back to the science vessel where he assembled his team in the conference room.

"Looks like my gamble paid off. Unlike our last excursion, this planet is not going to be so pleasant. But it's just the kind of place any self respecting Tabar Caluso could call home."

Ralston raised his hand. "Where do we search?"

"The trader gave me information of its last known coordinates. He said they frequent the same area. Shouldn't be too hard to find."

Marigold's was skeptical. "That is, if it turns out to be the right planet. And I have one more question. If this creature was so valuable, why didn't the trader sell it himself? I'm sure he could have made a nice profit."

"I paid him handsomely. He said he didn't want the fuss." Jason activated a monitor screen. "This is the only known picture of the elusive little bastard. As you can see, it's not much to look at. Pot belly, webbed feet and its gills on the neck filter the deadly gasses."

The lead veterinarian stood up. "I've prepared a holding tank on what limited knowledge we have about the creature's environment. It's basically an omnivore; consuming small insects and plants. I'm sending a team to gather some native fauna and foliage."

"Very well. Marigold and Ralston will split up in teams. Fully contained breathing suits. Any more questions? Kid gloves on this one. The Tabar Caluso is timid and delicate."

The teams transported to the planet in white suits and helmets. Ralston measured the temperature at 145 degrees. "Nice little vacation spot."

The veterinarians examined the ubiquitous large leafed reddish pink foliage as Ralston easily traversed the flattened landscape while crushing colonies of finger size maggots under his boots. Marigold, who was at least a mile away, contacted him. "Plenty of food for them."

"I don't see any other invertebrates."

"Me either. Keep in touch."

Ralston trekked across a field of smooth topped boulders and was surprised by a Tabar Caluso leisurely consuming a mouthful of maggots and pink leaves. He aimed his weapon, which was set on the lowest power level, fired one shot and the creature tipped over and fell to the ground. "This is Ralston. Target immobilized."

Jason responded. "Are you kidding me?"

"It was just eating there. I'm sending the coordinates."

"Phenomenal."

"Be honest, that was the easiest capture I've ever made."

The veterinarians, who had gathered a substantial amount of indigenous plants and insects, were beamed aboard the ship. When the Tabar Caluso had awoken from its unconscious state, it resumed eating as if nothing had happened. Jason and Marigold admired their new prize and couldn't wait to return to Earth.

The Captain of the Ellington was just about to order them back to home space when alarms went off and the shields were activated. "Drio vessel approaching fast."

"Where did it come from?"

"Must have been hidden on the other side of the planet. It's a class 4B cruiser. Minimal armaments."

"Hold steady in case they have company."

"Long range scans are negative."

"All right, let's see what they want."

The black ship with green emblems stopped directly in front of the much larger battleship. The view screen revealed one pilot, a Drio with bright yellow skin, a high forehead and black hair. "I apologize for the intrusion. My long range sensors indicated a large war vessel approaching. When I determined your place of origin, I revealed myself."

"Drio pilot, what business do you have here?"

"My name is Elomoros and I am not a military officer. This is obviously not a military vessel and I do not represent the Drio Empire."

"I find it difficult to believe a lone Drio vessel is this far away from home."

"I have the right to be in neutral space. I was searching for a female Tabar Caluso and I believe you have it."

"How would you know that?"

"I monitored your transport beam."

"What is it that you want?"

"The Tabar Caluso. You see, I've already captured a male of the species. I was searching for that female. Perhaps we can make a deal?"

"I'm not in a position to make any deals. However, I can put you through to the one that's in charge of this operation."

"Very well."

Jason appeared on the view screen. "Elomoros, is it? You want to make some kind of deal?"

"A trade is more like it."

"Trading away something as valuable as a Tabar Caluso seems remote."

"I suspect we are kindred spirits. Perhaps in your world our profession is respected. However, my race considers it mostly irrelevant. If I could bring home a mating pair of Tabar Caluso, it would greatly enhance my status." He paused and looked away for a moment. "I've been searching these systems for an entire month."

"I'm sorry that we found the creature, but I doubt you have anything worth trading. This is such a rare animal."

"Oh, but I do. Something far more valuable. Do you mind if I transport to your ship to discuss the terms?"

"Not at all. We'll beam you to our conference room."

"I'll have something with me. It's not dangerous."

"The transport filters will eliminate any undesirable elements."

Jason, Marigold and Ralston greeted the Drio pilot in the science vessel conference room. He brought a twelve inch high transparent jar and set it on the table. Jason curiously inspected it and saw what looked like a translucent milky green gelatinous blob. "What the hell is this?"

"The Drio confidently placed his hand on the top of the jar. "That, my friend, is a Dephalian."

"Never heard of it."

"I'm not surprised."

Ralston examined it closely. "Looks like a jelly fish."

"This is what you want to trade for?"

"This specimen is deceased. But yes, that's my deal. Or at least to divulge the planet where they come from."

Jason smiled sarcastically. "It'd better do a song and dance."

"I understand your pessimism. Especially for a dead specimen. But I assure you this is far more sophisticated than anything you've ever come across." He turned away and walked towards the window. "I'm going back to my ship. Have your scientists thoroughly examine it. I'll await your decision."

"I don't see much reason, but we'll take a peek."

"Feel free to dissect it."

He transported back to his vessel and Jason stared at them. "What do think?"

Marigold swiveled the jar on the table. "I don't know. He seemed pretty confident in his assertions."

The veterinarians placed the Dephalian in a stasis chamber, scrutinized it under a high powered microscope and used lasers to delicately slice it into pieces for various tests. Subjecting to every kind of spectral range, they were able to obtain a complete anatomical, chemical and biological map to the cellular level.

Jason reclined in his quarters and drank an alcoholic beverage he had brought from Earth. Drowsy, he was about to fall asleep when a frantic scientist contacted him. "Trumbel, get down here right away!"

"What's the matter?"

"Just come down to the lab immediately."

Jason swiftly made his way through the corridors and interrupted a group of highly animated scientists and veterinarians. "Well, what is it?"

The head scientist gawked at him. "This is the most amazing life form we have ever seen."

"That poor excuse for a piece of rubber?"

"You don't understand. We subjected it to every known test. This creature does not fit into any category of what we would consider a life form."

"Give it to me in layman's terms."

"The Dephalian is a plant eater. Actually, it uses a toxin to break down vegetable matter. But much like the termite can't digest wood; the Dephalian cannot digest the plant matter. But that's where the similarities differ from the termite, or any other species known. It appears to be asexual and does not have a symbiotic relationship with any host. It breaks down the plant life . . . and get ready for this. It transforms the plant matter into either animal fats or mineral deposits. Apparently it's able to digest those reconstituted elements."

"Ridiculous. What kind of thing eat rocks and meat?"

"This life form does in a round about way. It's incapable of directly absorbing meat protein or minerals. We determined that upon examination. But as long as there are plants, it will flourish. It has a very simple nervous system and no detectable intelligence."

"Is it dangerous?"

"Not unless you're a plant. Essentially we have a creature that is animal, vegetable and mineral. You have to bargain for the Dephalian. Trade everything we have for it if necessary."

"It's that important?"

"The most incredible find in zoological history."

"If that's the case, I know what I have to do."

Jason summoned the Drio pilot, who was the picture of arrogance. "I take it your scientists were impressed?"

"Where did you get this specimen?"

"The Dephalian was given to me by a merchant in the Kerivio system. At first I thought it was a hoax. How could this insignificant life form be so special? But when I had it tested, I had the same response you had. So I paid a large sum for a map of where to find them. I had just captured the male Tabar Caluso and was about to do the same with the female before proceeding to that source. Unfortunately for me, you came along and altered my plans."

"So I hand over the Tabar Caluso and we share the wealth?"

"Something like that."

"We'll have to verify everything first."

"Of course. I will guide you to their place of origin."

"Forgive me for being a little suspicious, but this planet wouldn't be near Drio space?"

"On the contrary, it's in the opposite direction. Much closer to your territorial space." He sighed. "Mr. Trumbel, I'm told your species has integrity. So I suggest we trust each other."

"Trust or no trust, just show us the proof."

"Mr. Trumbel, you shouldn't believe everything you've been told about my race. We are not barbarians."

"I don't care if your people feed your children to Saldosian snails. You just come through with the Dephalian."

"Very well. It's about twenty four of your hours from here."

Jason and Marigold cuddled in bed in their private quarters, having finally put aside time to make love. Jason, who was always self absorbed, could only speak about the expedition's overwhelming success. "Our Captain contacted the Drio Empire and they pretty much corroborated Elomoros' story. He's a bit of a pariah. They also had no problem with our venturing into Noma Six."

"And they shouldn't."

"Yep, things are really going our way." He sensed that Marigold was sulking. "What's the matter?"

"Oh, nothing."

He sat up. "Come on, Marigold. We've just been intimate and now you seem disappointed."

"Not in that. It's just the situation with Ralston."

"I see."

"Do you prefer his trapping methods over mine?"

Jason responded cautiously. "It's not that I prefer his methods over yours. I'll admit he's reckless. But sometimes you have to take chances. But there's no question that you're more seasoned than he is."

"I don't mean to complain."

He kissed her on the forehead. "Ralston reminds me of me when I was younger. I did stupid things, but got lucky."

"I don't like putting my team in harm's way." She ran her palm up and down his arm. "Maybe I'm just a little jealous."

"You shouldn't be. When I met you, I got a great wife and an expert trapper. How many men can brag about that?"

She smiled. "I'm concerned that pursuing the Dephalian will put the rest of the cargo at risk. We can always arrange a future expedition."

"We'll be all right. We'll collect the Dephalian and that should give us a week to make it back."

"It's cutting it close."

"Look, we have the Drio pilot with us now and he's directing us to the planet. I don't want to risk losing this opportunity."

"I understand."

Ralston waited patiently in the science vessel's transport bay. The on duty technician entered the sequence and a beautiful blond female military office with pinned up hair materialized on the pad. "Welcome aboard, Lieutenant Janice Evers."

"Why, thank you Ralston. Shall we proceed to the gymnasium?"

"This way."

They strode down the corridor side by side. "Your self defense lesson should be quite invigorating."

"When do you have to go back on duty?"

"Twelve hours."

"That should be enough for a complete session." He stopped at his quarters, opened the door and they both fell into a passionate kiss. "All right, Lieutenant, let's see what you got."

She disrobed and feverishly kissed his mouth and neck. "Oh, you're going to get the lesson of your life."

Ralston ushered her over to his bed. "You think you can teach me a thing or two?"

"Let's find out."

They collapsed on the bed and made love. After their exhaustive encounter, they nestled up to each other.

"Was I military enough for you?"

She smiled and playfully slapped his arm. "You were magnificent."

"Well thank you."

"I bet you do this kind of thing often."

"Do you mean do I have a woman in every port?"

"Do you?"

He was reluctant. "I'd be lying if I said I didn't. But you're certainly my first military officer. I never had much interest in the military up until now."

"The military's my whole life. Father, mother, sister."

He saluted. "Wow."

"Not interested in the rigors of military discipline? What would you say to just plain old discipline?"

"I'd say bring it on."

The Ellington Captain was called to the Bridge when long range sensors detected an armada of small vessels. The Drio pilot signaled them. "I failed to mention that this region has its share of marauders. They're a lose confederation and not a threat to you."

"I still would have preferred to have that information."

"I will engage them if you wish."

"We'll take care of it. Stand by." The Captain turned to his ordinance officer. "Scan the marauders. I want to know what we're up against."

"Yes, Captain." He completed the scans and shook his head. "They're no match for us. Six of our fighters should suffice."

"Very well. Send them out. Defensive posture unless engaged."

The fighters jettisoned out of the dock and angled towards the enemy armada. When they were within range, seventy five vessels attacked them with a barrage of lasers and cannon fire. The commander ordered minimum retaliation with a series of shots to their engines. After disabling one third of their vessels, the remainder of them fled and the fighters returned safely to the Ellington.

"Well done." The Captain spoke to the helmsman. "Resume course."

A few hours later they reduced to sub-light speed and into a solar system with two gas giants and three solid spheres. Ralston prepared for the excursion with a bevy of ropes and pulleys. Marigold strolled into the locker room. "Looks like you're ready for a mountain climb."

"They tell me we can just pick these things off the ground. If that's the case, I might as well get some exercise."

"We don't have enough time for that. We have to get back to Earth."

Ralston stared at her oddly. "I'm curious, Marigold. I made a pass at you a year before you met Jason."

"What of it?"

"You remember what you told me? You said I was too young for you. Yet you married a man much older than yourself."

"You want me to say that your offer was tempting? Okay, it was. But I always had Jason in my sights."

"All those exciting adventures he wrote about?"

"They were intoxicating."

Ralston shoved the supplies in his back pack. "Don't ever tell him I said this. But I think he was the best there ever was."

"No chance of that. Jason's ego doesn't need stroking."

The Ellington Captain was alerted by the navigator. "Target planet in site."

"Affrimative. Notify Trumbel and Elomoros."

The purplish, green planet was about three quarters the size of Earth and contained more rivers and lakes than oceans. The scans indicated that it had a breathable atmosphere with elevated oxygen content. Jason assembled his team in the transporter bay where the Drio pilot and the Ellington's second officer had just materialized.

"Welcome everyone. This is the last stop on what has been an extremely successful and profitable journey. I want to thank my staff, the battleship crew and of course Elomoros for making this possible. The Ellington's second officer will now address you."

"The atmosphere is breathable. There are no dangerous elements. The temperatures in the target zone are about seventy degrees. Other than vegetation and insect life, there appears to be no other life forms; with the exception of the Dephalian, which are mainly concentrated in one particular area."

Ralston raised his hand. "No other life forms on a planet like this? I find that unusual."

"Our sensors have shown massive debris and rubble from what must have been an extinct civilization from twenty thousand years ago. Judging from the devastation, we believe they had some kind of planetary disaster or war. There are no buildings or structures left to make that determination."

Jason draped his arms around his wife's shoulders. "So that's it. Let's prepare for transport. I've separated the teams so you won't get in each other's way. Marigold's team will retrieve the Dephalian and Ralston's team will gather the plants. Are there any more questions? Mr. Max?"

"Yeah. If I find a big hairy beast, I'll bring it back for lunch."

You heard the second officer. There's nothing else down there. We need to make this quick and get back to Earth." He glanced at Elomoros. "Once you retrieve your specimens, you're welcome to the Tabar Caluso."

"It's been a pleasure doing business with you."

"You did well. Maybe this will bring our civilizations closer."

"That would be excellent. But as I told you before, my government doesn't think much about me."

Marigold's team beamed down to a valley with numerous ponds and lakes where vast colonies of Dephalians feasted on the abundant foliage. The veterinarians were equipped with rubber gloves, metal boxes, gripping tongs and spatulas for the collection of the docile, slow moving species.

"There's certainly a lot of them."

The lead veterinarian issued orders. "Now we don't know how fragile they are. So use great care. Try not to handle them directly."

Marigold nodded. "They move like starfish, so we won't have any trouble gathering them. Let's proceed."

Jason contacted Marigold. "The Tabar Caluso has been safely transported to the Drio vessel. Elomoros sends his best."

"I wonder how Ralston's doing with the plants?"

"I'm sure he hates it with every fiber of his body."

Ralston's team was a quarter mile away from Marigold. Although the veterinarians concluded that any vegetable matter would suffice, their instructions were to select only three types of plants. The team was able to secure full grown specimens, as well as seeds for future growing. As they toiled, Ralston was distracted by the sound of rushing water just over a short ridge line. "I'm going to do a little exploring. You can handle it from here."

The veterinarian was concerned. "All right, but we need to get back to the ship as soon as possible."

"I know. We're still on schedule. If anything comes up, call me."

An experienced climber, Ralston chose the simplest route to the top. Once at the precipice, he overlooked a violent, misty waterfall crashing down on multiple boulders. He hoofed it swiftly down the other side of the graduated slope and into the thick foliage below. He hiked along a turbulent stream to the base of the waterfall, feeling a powerful vibration under the slippery rocks. Enjoying the magnificent scenery, he carefully stepped over and around the boulders, halting his progress when the relentless mist forced him back.

He waited for a few minutes, turned around and then headed back towards the ridge. Suddenly and without warning, he fell through a heavily covered patch of ground and plummeted down a vertical twenty foot wall of rocks and plants. He knocked his head against the hardened ground and laid there with hazy vision and a pounding headache. He tried to communicate with his team, but his equipment had malfunctioned. He pushed himself up, but immediately collapsed into unconsciousness.

When Marigold had been unsuccessful in her attempts to contact him, she notified the Ellington Bridge. Unable to locate his signal, they scanned the surface for all the heat signatures and accounted for every team member except Ralston. When all the teams arrived back on the science vessel, Jason and Marigold notified the Captain.

"When was the last time you saw him", he asked?

"Actually, I didn't. The veterinarian said he went exploring."

Jason interrupted. "That still doesn't explain why we can't locate his heat signature."

"That is puzzling. He could be in a cave. We do have the means to find personnel under these conditions. But we'd have to have more specificity."

Jason was angry. "Just what I needed. We got to get this cargo back to Earth. I got a good mind to leave him here."

Marigold was incensed. "We can't do that."

"I know. But I can fire him."

"I have a suggestion."

"I'm all ears, Captain."

We'll escort the science vessel back to Earth and leave six fighters here with a search party. That should be enough to deter any marauders. I don't think they'll attack again, but we'll be ready for them."

"Sounds reasonable."

"Jason, I'm going to stay and look for him."

"Good. And when you find him, tell him thanks."

"Don't worry. I'll get him back."

The Ellington and the science vessel accelerated to warp speed and left behind six fighters, a shuttle, Marigold and ten soldiers. They quickly mapped a standard search pattern around the area he had disappeared. Marigold was transported to the top of the ridge and beheld the impressive waterfall. Two more soldiers were within sight of her and began to call out his name.

Marigold was unaware that she was dangerously close to the pit that he had fallen into. Ralston had fully regained consciousness and heard her voice. Still wobbly and disorientated, he stood up slowly and called out to her. She was barely able to hear him over the thunderous crash of the waterfall. "Where the hell are you?"

"Down here!"

She noticed a hole in the vegetation that must have been opened where he fell though. She bent down on her knees and flashed a light to the bottom. "Are you all right?"

"Yeah. Banged up, but in one piece. My communication device is inoperative. Scanners, too."

Marigold contacted the nearby soldiers to assist her and ordered the others back to the shuttle. "I'm giving them your coordinates."

He touched some blood on his scalp. "Make it fast."

The soldiers were unable to contact the orbiting ships. Frustrated, Marigold shouted down to him. "We'll have to lift you out."

"Fine by me."

They tied a rope to a tree trunk and hoisted her over the edge and into the pit. She briefly examined him and didn't find any broken bones. She aimed her scanner along the rock wall. "This is very unusual. I believe it's some kind of artificial structure. At least the remains of one."

"What do you mean?"

"That must have been why we couldn't locate you. These walls are made up of a thick, unknown material. Nothing like I've ever seen before. This place must have been some kind of a bunker or shelter. It shielded your heat signature and that's why we probably couldn't get your signal."

"The former civilization must have built it."

"That would be my guess."

"Hey, my spotlight works." He lit up an overgrown stand of bushes and noticed something shiny on the other side. "What the hell's this?"

"What do you see?"

He cleared out the brush and shined his light on sophisticated equipment lined up against the far wall of the pit. "Looks like some of their technology survived."

Marigold ordered the soldiers to stand by. She then scanned the equipment. "There's still power in there."

"You're kidding. From twenty thousand year ago?"

"Apparently so. There's a monitor screen. Let's see if we can activate it."

Elomoros had returned to his home world and was greeted honorably by the ruling council. He stood before a half circle of podiums. "Commander, I trust you were successful?"

"Yes, my lords."

"And our breeding pair of Tabar Caluso?"

"They have been safely returned to their keepers. They proved to be excellent bait."

"Your report?"

"They accepted my story and collected the Dephalians. Our intelligence was correct. They intend to bring the entire cargo back to Earth. In the confusion, one of their colleagues was lost and some of their vessels remained behind. But our forces dispensed with them before they could contact their home world."

"You are certain these Dephalians were immature?"

"Yes, my lords. I guided them to the watery lowlands."

"You have served the Empire with distinction. That is why the Drio have always maintained superiority over its enemies."

Marigold was able to restart the ancient power generator. The console lit up with flickering lights and then a visual recording. The indigenous race were humanoid, but with knobby facial features and upward sloping scalps. A male of the species spoke in an unknown language. Ralston shook his head. "Wish I knew what he was saying."

"United Earth translators would be useless without past references."

"Let's see what's going on."

They watched the humanoid point to an illustrated diagram of Dephalians and what appeared to be groups of them in different categories originating from one single species. The other scientists in the room seem to be worried. Marigold proceeded to the next transmission. "See what else we have."

"This is bizarre."

They recognized the same individual in a laboratory with several other scientists, technicians and a heavily fortified transparent booth harboring Dephalians. The scientists attempted to subject them to an intense light and then to frigid temperatures. None of these techniques seem to have any effect, but they kept trying.

"I wish I knew what they were saying."

"Ralston, look at that. They're panicking."

"Why? Nothing's happening."

She shook her head. "No, something's happening."

The Dephalians suddenly grew in size and melted through the outer structure. As the lab crew fled for their lives, some of the Dephalians dissolved their flesh, while others passed through solid walls like butter. The transmission ended.

Ralston squeezed his laser holster. "Those diagrams. They were reproduction tables. This bunker must have been a last refuge."

Marigold was horrified. "When they reproduce they must be able to consume everything. These people weren't destroyed by war."

"And we just sent them all back to Earth."

The soldiers above began screaming and Marigold and Ralston ran up to the wall. She shouted up to them, but there was no response. They heard rustling above and backed away. An enlarged Dephalian leaned over the edge of the pit, slithered down the side of the wall and dropped in front of them. They removed their pistols and fired, but the light beams passed right through it. Now resembling a cone shaped mass, the Dephalian glided towards them aggressively.

"Goodbye, Marigold."

"But Ralston . . . ?"

WEDDING

Handsome by any standard, Jim Dunning opened his eyes. Head buried in a fluffy pillow and vision blurred, he had no idea of his surroundings. He tried to move, but was jolted by a pounding headache that left him breathless. Unaware of what had happened the previous night, a sweet delectable odor indicated the presence of a female. He turned his head and didn't recognize her; but there was no mistaking dowdiness. Contently snoring, she was somewhat plump with a rounded face, flat nose and smallish eyes. Jim's only thought was to get out of bed without waking her. He gingerly peeled off the blanket, eased his torso to the side, planted his feet on the floor and pushed himself off the mattress, mindful of every squeak. He gathered his clothes and brought them into the living room where he dressed, slipped on his shoes, unlocked the apartment door and shut it quietly behind him. Still nauseous, he crept down the hallway and out onto the street where he called a taxi service that brought him home. He was grateful that it was Sunday, allowing him a full day to recuperate before going back to work.

On Monday Jim had recovered from his alcoholic binge and managed to get to work a half an hour before starting time. He had respectable employment at a marketing agency and secluded himself in his office as the other employees intermittently arrived. Soon the coffee pots percolated, the donut boxes appeared, finger's taped on keyboards and muted voices gossiped from behind neck high cubicles.

Jim saved a computer file, leaned back in his chair and stretched his arms well behind his head. Yawning, he wandered out of his office and met up with his good friend and co-worker. "Well, if it isn't lover boy."

Jim raised his palm authoritatively. "Not now."

"Put on quite a show Saturday night."

"I don't remember much about it."

"With the exception of that young lady you left with."

Jim clutched onto his friend's arms and turned him away from the main floor. "Who else knows about this?" He glanced over his shoulders and noticed everyone was staring. "Oh great."

"I wasn't the only one there, you know."

He dragged him into his office, shut the door and plunged onto his chair. "I made a mistake. One lousy mistake."

"Who said it was a mistake? You two were meant for each other. The night was old, plenty of tequila and you were willing."

"That's just it. Why was I willing?"

"You drank, buddy. You were pretty whacked."

"How could I have let myself get that wasted?"

"Hey, it happens. Don't sweat it."

"Don't sweat it? Look what happened."

"Oh yeah . . . woof."

He swiveled nervously in his chair. "This will never happen again. From now on, it's going to be just one beer."

"You expect me to believe that?"

With the exception of a few periodic taunts, Jim survived the rest of the day without getting sick. Before leaving the office he checked his schedule, saved his files, turned off the computer and closed the lights. He drove home to his condominium, opened the mailbox and perused through bills and magazines on his way up the elevator. About to enter his unit, he noticed the front door was slightly ajar. Adrenaline pumping, he cautiously entered the foyer and the living room lights were on. Ready to bolt out the door and call the police, he sniffed a familiar pleasant odor.

"Who's in here?"

"Hello, Jim"

The woman that he had slept with from the club walked out into the middle of his living room. Incensed, he circled her in a wide berth. "What the hell are you doing here?"

"Sally. My name is Sally."

"How did you get in? This is a security building."

"You didn't say anything when you left."

He superficially eyed the room to see if anyone else was there. "How did you find me, anyway?"

"Hello! Your wallet. Your driver's license."

He nodded dismally. "Oh, yeah. But that doesn't change anything. You have to leave. You do understand that you're breaking and entering?"

"I'm sorry you feel that way."

"Sally, is it? I'm sure you're a nice girl. But you don't want anything to do with me. I'm terrible in relationships."

"I don't care, Jim. When you made love to me, it was magical. You took me to a place I've never been before. Our love was sublime."

"You got this all wrong. What we had was one night. And maybe I was good, though I can't imagine under those conditions. But it's not the real thing."

"Jim, I'm in love with you."

He paced in front of the couch. "This is crazy. You can't be in love with me. Not after one night."

"But I am."

"Sally, you're going to have to leave or I'm calling the police."

She crossed her beady eyes. "How can you say that? I love you. I want to marry you."

"Marry me! That's it, I'm calling the cops."

"All right, I'll go. But I'm in love with you and I want to get married. I know in my heart you feel the same way."

He reached into his coat, removed his cell phone and took a picture of her. "I don't want any trouble. It's been nice knowing you."

Sally reluctantly departed and Jim fell back against the door and hoped this would be his last encounter with her. That evening he had a restless sleep and woke up every hour. By morning he was exhausted, but still had to go to work. Once there, he remained in his office and tried to have as little interaction with others as possible.

In the early afternoon he was distracted by a commotion on the main floor. A few female employees were gathered around something hidden from his view.

"What the hell?" He dashed out of his office and couldn't believe that Sally had a wedding dress draped over each arm. "This can't be." He yanked her aside forcefully. "What are you doing here?"

"I'm getting opinions on my dresses."

"You must be a certified nut." He noticed some of the female employees were discreetly chuckling. "This is my place of work."

"I thought you'd want to involve your friends?"

One of the clerks interrupted facetiously. "Yeah Jim, your bride wants help."

"She's not my bride."

Another female pointed. "I like that one better, Sally."

"Really? Cause I feel the same way."

Jim slapped his forehead. "There's not going to be any wedding." He roughly shoved the dresses back into the boxes. "Sally, you have to go."

Another female playfully mocked him. "Come on Jim, get with the program."

He took Sally by the wrist and led her to his office. "Are you out of your mind? This is harassment."

"Jim, you seem disappointed. It's our wedding."

"It's not our wedding. I don't want to marry you. You have to get this through your thick skull, I don't love you."

"But I love you, Jim. I want to be Sally Dunning."

"That's not going to happen." Jim feigned a sympathetic tone. "Look, Sally. I'm sure you're a nice girl and there's somebody out there for you. But it's just not me. Can't you understand that?"

"I don't believe you feel that way."

"Just get your dresses and go before I have to contact security."

"I'll go, if that's what you want. I guess I'll have to make the decision on the dress myself." She picked up the boxes, tucked them under her armpits and strolled towards the elevator.

The staff retreated behind their cubicles and Jim got a call from his mother on his cell phone. He reluctantly answered it. "Hi, mom."

"Jimmy, where have you been? You're not returning my calls."

"Sorry, haven't been checking my messages."

"The flight comes in tonight."

He snapped his fingers. "The flight."

"Is something wrong?"

"No, nothing's wrong. Aunt Miranda still picking you up?"

"Yes. I just spoke to her an hour ago."

"Good. Then I'll see you Friday."

"I can't wait." There was a pause on the line. "Are you sure you're okay? You sound funny."

"Everything's fine, mom. Say hi to Aunt Miranda."

With his mother coming to visit and his boss admonishing him to keep his personal affairs away from the workplace, Jim wondered if his life could get any worse. Even his friend, who had originally found humor in the whole affair, began to feel sorry and embarrassed for him. He now realized that Sally was not going to be out of his life so easily.

Jim had arranged to pick his mother up Friday night for a dinner at an expensive restaurant. When he knocked on his aunt's door, his mother greeted him with a powerful hug and looped her arm inside his. "How's my genius doing?"

"Great. So how's dad doing?"

"You know dad. Sits at home, watches TV and makes his models."

"He likes to do those things. There's nothing wrong with that."

Her face soured. "He's impossible."

"You always say that."

"Any girl in your life I need to know about?"

"No!" he abruptly responded.

"Gheesh . . . just asking. I'm not getting any younger. I want grandkids one day."

"Mom, I just haven't met the right person."

Aunt Miranda interrupted them. "Come on you two, be nice. You only see each other a couple times year."

"You're right, aunty. Sure you don't want to join us?"

"You two have a lot to talk about. I can see you anytime."

Jim had reservations at a seafood restaurant and they were guided to an exceptional table with a view of the harbor. They ordered exotic drinks and caught up on family news like Uncle Bart's toe fungus, Aunt Jill's tiresome complaints, Cousin Tim's basement antics, Cousin Mary's flatulence and Uncle Herbert's long overdue fifty-five year retirement.

For the entrée the waiter carried out trays of Australian lobster tails and seared halibut; of which they consumed all but a few morsels. And then for some reason Jim peered over his mother's shoulder and was dumbfounded when he saw Sally heading for the table. His face almost hit the plate. "Oh, no, this can't be."

"What's the matter, Jimmy?"

"This is not happening."

His mother turned around. "Who's this?"

"No one, mom. Nobody."

Sally extended her hand. "Is this your mother, Jim?"

Jim stood up angrily and squeezed Sally's forearm. "What are you doing here?"

"I wanted to see you."

Unaware of the situation, Jim's mother tried to be cordial. "Is this a friend of yours?"

"No. She's not a friend. More like a pest."

Sally frowned. "How can you say that?"

The disturbance brought the manager over to the table. "Is there a problem?"

"Yes. This woman is bothering us."

The manager turned to Sally. "Madam, you'll have to leave."

"But this is my boyfriend, soon to be my husband."

Jim's mother gawked at Sally and turned pale. Jim faced the manager and pretended to pull out his hair. "Get her out of here."

"You'll have to come with me or I will be forced to call the authorities."

Dejected, she followed the manager out between the tables as patrons snappishly commented. Jim held out his hands. "I don't know what to say, mom. We had one date and this girl's been stalking me ever since."

"She must be a very troubled individual."

"She even came to my job."

"We have to do something about this. You and I are going down to the police station and get a restraining order. That should take care of her."

"I think you're right. But you don't have to go, mom."

She gently rubbed his cheek. "Of course I do. I'm your mother."

There was only one citizen filling out a complaint at the front desk of the police station when Jim and his mother walked inside. Another officer beckoned them over. "Can I help you?"

"My son's being harassed by this woman."

"What woman?"

Jim spoke up. "Her name is Sally."

"Last name?"

"I don't know."

The police officer stared impatiently. "Where does she live?"

"I'm not sure. But I know the building."

"Look, sir. I have to have a last name, or some kind of information."

Jim showed the officer an image of Sally on his cell phone. "This is what she looks like."

The officer winced. "Oooh, I see. But we can't fill out a restraining order without more information."

"I understand. I'm sure I'll be able to get more soon." His mother insisted that the officer fill out the report, but Jim prodded her to leave. "I'll take care of it. I know what I have to do, mom."

"But you need protection."

"Don't worry, she's not hostile. Just a little psychotic."

Jim drove his mother backed to his aunt's home and returned to his condo. Half expecting to find Sally, he was relieved that the condo was undisturbed. It was only a matter of thirty minutes later that he heard a knock on the door. He looked through the peep hole, immediately called the police, opened the door and invited her inside.

"I missed you, Jim. Your mother seemed nice."

"I'm glad you came over."

"You think she liked me? It's important that she likes me."

"You made quite an impression."

Sally relaxed on the couch in the living room. "I wanted to ask you about the arrangements. Do you want to get married in a church?"

"Churches are good." Jim stared at the clock and soon the police arrived at the front door. He immediately pointed to Sally. "This woman is harassing me. I want her out and I want a restraining order."

"Do you have identification, Miss?"

She handed him a driver's license and he wrote the information down. She seemed confused. "What's this all about? Jim and I are in love."

"Miss, you're not allowed to harass people. Is this your current address?"

"Yes."

"You'll have to come with us."

Resigned to her fate, Sally edged towards the door. "Jim, are you really going to let them take me?"

"You bet I am. I hope this makes everything perfectly clear. I don't ever want to see you again."

"But our wedding?"

"There's not going to be a wedding. I don't love you and I don't want you."

"I'm disappointed, Jim. We could have had something worth while."

"All I want is my life back." He shut the door behind them and raised his fist in the victory salute.

Now that Sally had been dealt with, Jim was ready to frequent his old haunts. Jim met up with a few friends and visited several nightclubs. He drank less alcohol, danced a little more than usual and was more leery about the women he met. Instinctively checking to see if Sally was around, he felt comfortable again engaging women that showed an interest in him. He was no longer worried that he could end up dating another Sally.

One evening Jim was playing poker at a friend's house when his luck ran out. Sober and two hundred dollars poorer, he ambled towards his parked car and was distracted by a black SUV that screeched around the corner of the block and skidded to a stop right next to him. The door opened and two muscular men forcefully pulled him inside. The vehicle's tires spun and they drove away at high speeds.

Jim immediately recognized that his four captors had a family resemblance to Sally. "What do you guys want?"

The man in the passenger seat turned around. "You Jim Dunning?"

"No. I'm Tom Mac ... mac ... ca ... "

"Yeah, you're Dunning. Sally told us you were here."

He squirmed in his seat. "This is kidnapping."

"We're not playing games."

"I don't know what you guys want, but like I told Sally, I'm not interested in a relationship."

"Not my problem, pal. All I know is that Sally wants you."

Jim began to surmise this ordeal may not end well. "I'm sorry she feels that way. But come on, guys. I don't love her."

The man sitting adjacent to him scoffed. "This guy's nothing."

Jim anxiously agreed. "Nothing. You're absolutely right. I'm nothing. Sally deserves better."

"Damn right she does."

The black SUV turned into a debris filled alley and rolled to a stop between two brick buildings and a high chain link fence. "Why are we here?

"Get out."

Leg's shaky and bladder about to burst, Jim meekly exited the vehicle and was surrounded by the four men. The implication of the dead end and its numerous trash bins played on his fears. "Let's talk about this. What can I do to convince you I'm not right for Sally?"

The driver pounded his fist into his other hand. "We know you're not right for our Sally. She can do much better."

"So you're going to kill me?"

The driver walked over to a drain pipe fastened to a brick wall and slowly tore it away from its fetters, crumpled it up into a pretzel shape and tossed it to the ground. Jim watched in disbelief as another man placed both hands on the edge of a metal trash bin and ripped it down the middle as if it were paper. He fell to his knees and pleaded. "I don't want to die."

The driver shook his head. "Enough of this theater. We're not going to kill you. Sally wouldn't like that."

Jim's sniveling abated. "What kind of people are you? I know you're not human."

"We're all members of the same clan. Sally is one of us. It just so happens that her father is one of the elders." He was obviously thinking about something else. "But there may be a way we can get you out of this."

"Anything. I'll do anything."

The driver poked his finger into Jim's chest. "If you can convince Sally's father that she's too good for you, maybe you got a chance."

"I can do that. Believe me, I'm no good."

"Dunning, you don't have to convince us. Her father already has a very low opinion of you."

Jim stood up. "Then what are we waiting for?"

They nodded simultaneously. "Get in."

The black SUV whipped around the corner of the alley and maintained a lawful speed throughout the city limits. Once on the highway they increased their speed to eighty miles per hour. "So, where are we going?"

"Better make yourself comfortable. We have a long ride ahead of us. We don't live in nice little suburbs."

As the sun started to rise, Jim's throat was dry and his stomach was grumbling. "Don't you guys ever eat or drink?"

"Hey, lover boy's hungry." They noticed a fast food joint off the side of the highway and the SUV entered the drive thru lane.

Jim ordered a cheeseburger, fries and malt and started devouring them. "You guys aren't eating?"

Their faces distorted. "We don't consume dead meat."

"Funny, I never pictured you as vegetarians."

Hours later the vehicle slowed down and made a left turn onto a partially paved road that led up to the base of a small mountain range. At first the truck pitched and bounced over divots and holes, sending the occupants careening against the side panels. And then without explanation the ride leveled out and felt like they were on a cushion of air over what appeared to be difficult terrain. What Jim didn't know was that the four tires had retracted and the vehicle was levitating off the ground.

When the SUV drifted off the road and easily maneuvered over scattered boulders and desert shrubbery, Jim now understood he was traveling in a technologically advanced craft. The vehicle suddenly shot up a thousand feet, cleared a mountain ridge and dipped nose first down the other side. As they decelerated, a village appeared on each side of a narrow stream. The truck wheels extended and touched down next to a community with modern habitats that had unusual shapes.

Once outside the truck, Jim finally had a chance to stretch his muscles. And then Sally ran up to him and threw her arms around his shoulders. "Jim, you came."

"I didn't have much of a choice."

She led him away. "Come on, let's go see Poppa."

"Now's as good a time as any."

Other clan members surrounded them as Sally brought Jim to one of the larger structures. An older man emerged to greet them and Jim recognized the family resemblance. "Poppa, this is the man I love."

The elder gazed upon him with contempt. "You fell in love with this human?" He shook his head. "Oh, the youth of today."

"Isn't he dreamy?"

"I wouldn't put it that way."

Jim extended his hand. "How are you, sir?"

"Not happy that my daughter finds you so attractive."

"Believe me, I feel the same way."

"Sally, why don't you leave us? Jim and I need to talk."

"All right, Poppa. Don't hurt him."

"Come in to my abode, Dunning."

Jim surveyed the interior decorated with unusual objects that glowed, hummed and projected holograms in various parts of the room. "Of all the females you could have chosen from among your own kind, you wanted my daughter."

"Well to be technically correct, sir. I didn't pursue the relationship. You see, I'm no good for her. You don't want somebody like me as a son-in-law."

"Tell me about it. That's why you're here."

"Sally should find somebody better suited to her. Like one of your kind."

"Easier said than done. My wife and I are very upset about all this But there's a problem. We are a species that honor the choices of the individual rather than that of the family."

"Sir, you have to convince Sally I'm not the one for her. I don't know what else to say."

"It's getting dark soon. Join me outside."

"I'm not in love her. Shouldn't that be enough? It's your daughter's life we're talking about."

"Every father wants what's best for his daughter. But when that doesn't happen, sometimes we must accept it."

Jim's knees buckled. "If you don't mind me asking, where do you people come from?"

He pointed up to the sky where a few stars intermittently sparkled across the dwindling light of day. "We come from well beyond those stars. We are nomads. We stay, and then we move on. We are by definition, humanoid. We have the ability to manipulate our genetic composition to resemble many of the species we visit. How I appear to you now is a result of that ability."

"I don't care where you're from. Please stop this marriage."

He began to laugh. "Do you know how old Sally is? Two hundred of your Earth years. I am considerably older. And it's not unprecedented for one of our kind to fall in love with an indigenous species. That's what happened to Sally. Whether you like it or not, you captured her heart."

"But I didn't mean to."

"We've been here for twenty five years. I purchased this land legitimately and we are law abiding taxpayers. Most of us decide to live amongst each other. But there are some of us that choose to live among humans. Sally just wanted to fit in; find a job, become part of your society. We didn't discourage her." He led him to the center of the village. "I'm afraid you're going to be joining the family, Jim. And there's nothing you or I can do about that."

"But they said you could help?"

"Sally's in love and you must accept that."

"But I can't."

"I thought you might feel that way. It appears you need a little demonstration." The elder snapped his fingers and the villagers brought out a human citizen dressed in overalls."

"Who's that guy?"

"Just somebody that caused us some problems. I thought you might be curious about what we really look like." The elder's body slumped over; his fingers extended twelve inches from his hand and out of his mouth came a protruding stem with a hub of rotating teeth. Jim stumbled backwards as the other villagers transformed, pounced on the man and ripped him apart as bone fragments and shredded clothes floated to the ground. One of them snatched up a bone splinter, walked over to Jim and picked his teeth with it.

Sally's father morphed back into his human form. "Well son, it looks like you have two choices here."

Jim stood motionless with a sickened grin plastered on his face.

Church bells clanged, a limousine was parked on the street and a flood of guests took their seats in the pews. It was a beautiful sunny day as the bride and her father were poised to walk down the garland draped aisle. The groom and the best man stood at the front of the altar just as the organ music began to play. The bridesmaids were first to parade between the guests.

Jim's best man leaned over to him. "What do you think of your bride?"

"Like my electrolysis bill is going to bankrupt me."

"At least she smells great."

"Yeah, there's always that."

As the bride proceeded down the aisle, her family commented on how lovely she appeared. On the other side of the aisle, Jim's family and friends sat quietly with mortified expressions, stiffened shoulders and eyes staring straight forward. Sally parted ways with her father and joined her groom in front of the Minister, who called for the ring. Jim's heart beat rapidly and he even noticed that the Minister hesitated when pronouncing them man and wife.

When they were alone in their penthouse hotel room, Jim reclined on the bed and waited for his bride to return from the bathroom. She entered the room in a lace gown, accompanied by that enticing odor that permeated from her species. "You look . . . great."

"Thank you, Jim. "I'm going to make you very happy tonight."

"I'm sure you will." He patted the mattress. "Come on over here."

"Don't think you're going to get much sleep tonight, Jim Dunning."

He sat up. "So was I really that good?"

"I wonder how many children we're going to have."

That sidelined him. "Our species can breed?"

She pulled the covers up and over her. "Of course. But my gestation is four months shorter than humans."

"We'll have some explaining to do."

"That shouldn't be a problem. We'll just make up some kind of story that I didn't show."

"Works for me."

She snuggled up to him. "I love you."

"I still can't get over how good you smell."

"It's just my physiology."

"It's a bonus; believe me."

Several months later Sally gave birth to twins. Never imaging that this would happen in his life so soon, Jim quickly learned how to deal with pooping and incessant crying. He shared feeding and diaper duties and carried his offspring around the room to tire them out. He even admired Sally's motherly skills; though he'd still give up marriage for his freedom.

One evening while Sally was in the kitchen cleaning up after dinner, Jim was in the living room feeding one of the twins. He shoved the baby food in his son's mouth and burped him over his shoulder. After a few more spoonfuls, the baby puked and he grabbed a small towel to wipe his chin. Jim then swung his head towards the kitchen and was obviously in pain.

"Honey, the kids bite!"

SPECTATOR

R oss and Jenny, eighteen year old high school lovers, relished their summer days at the little lake just beyond town. As long as they could remember they were inseparable, having similar interests in sports, music and outdoor activities. So it was a forgone conclusion they would be attending the same university. Ross, the only child of a single father of few means, had earned a place in college with excellent grades and a baseball scholarship. On the other hand Jenny came from privilege and along with her well connected father and good grade point average had easily gained acceptance. On this humid day they found privacy under a lofty shade tree and reminisced about past summers together.

Having long argued who had the better fishing skills, Ross appreciated that Jenny was game for any spontaneous adventure. They had often hiked for days in the wilderness, but this was just another lazy afternoon with fishing poles, an ice chest and a bag of beef jerky.

Ross fastened a worm to his line. "Anything yet?"

Jenny shook her head, puffing away loose strands of hair stuck to the sides of her mouth. "I think it's too hot for fishing."

"They're out there. Got to be patient"

"I had a strike earlier."

He cast his line into the water. "Let the pro show you how it's done."

She giggled. "Yeah, sure."

A few minutes later Jenny's pole dipped sharply and the reel spun out. "Hooked."

He rolled his eyes. "Figures."

She wrestled the fish up to the bank, lifted it out of the water and held up a one pound bass.

"That's a beauty."

"You were saying something about being a pro?"

"I had to shoot my mouth off."

Jenny unhooked the fish and gently returned it to the lake. "Jenny one, Ross zero."

They fished for another hour and then withdrew to the blanket laid out under the shade. Rummaging through the ice chest, Ross pulled out two apple juices and a plastic tub of carrot sticks. Across the lake the sunlight burned bright orange, flickering through the tree leaves on its way to set. Ross stretched out on the blanket and Jenny tucked herself inside his chest.

"I'm going to miss this place."

"Do you think we'll find something like it at college?"

Jenny kissed him on the cheek. "If we do, I'm sure it will be crowed with thousand of kids looking for the same thing."

"Yeah. Really."

"I think of this place when I'm sad. It makes me feel better."

"You're not going to have enough time to be sad. Once we're at school, it's going to be go, go, go."

"That's right. All that studying."

"All that partying."

She slapped his arm. "They'll be none of that, Ross Kellon. No hussy's going to sweep you off your feet."

He sat up rigidly. "Me? What about you? I got to worry about some guy picking you up."

She smiled demurely and brushed her hand across his forehead. "You have nothing to worry about. I'm yours forever."

He stood up and grunted. "I got to take a piss."

"You're such a romantic."

Ross headed into the woods and pulled down his shorts. He was about to relieve himself and was distracted by something glittery under the dirt and vegetation. He stooped over and noticed the protruding edge of a golden object buried in the ground. He fell to his knees, dug it out with his fingers and held up a perfectly round disc that felt heavier than it appeared.

He brought it out to Jenny, who was rubbing sunscreen on her arms. "Hey babe, look what I found."

"What is it?"

"I don't know." He waved it around. "It's too big to be a DVD. Maybe it's one of those old laser records."

"I don't think so." She reached up and examined it. "This is like some kind of technology." She handed it back to him.

"Might be valuable."

A mild tremor reverberated through his hand. He stared oddly at the disc and then it wobbled violently. He released it, but it quickly rose upwards about eye level and hung motionless in mid-air. Jenny leaped to her feet and a blue light shot out from the disc. Before they could react or utter a word, they were transported to a medical laboratory aboard an extraterrestrial vessel where they observed dozens of short, squatty creatures with gray skin, large bulbous heads and pointed ears awkwardly bumping into each other. The creatures were clothed in silver garments with hardened shoulder extensions and seem to be focusing on a table in the central area where two other aliens were kept in restraints. To their horror, Ross and Jenny could hear them crying out and begging for mercy.

Squinting with pleasure, one of the creatures carried a drill with a saw blade over to the male and began cutting into his leg. He shouted in what must have been unbearable pain as the creatures seem to delight in the geysers of blood streaming from his body.

The male pleaded between cries of agony as another creature severed the arm of the female. He tried to protest, but could only manage a desperate whisper.

The terrified female screamed as another creature jabbed a thick needle into her eyeball. Unable to move, Jenny and Ross were somehow compelled to witness the carnage. The aliens jockeyed within the confines of the laboratory, positioning themselves over their victims while taking turns inflicting pain. One of them poured a vat of liquid over the male's face, which boiled away in seconds. The creatures somehow became aware of Ross and Jenny's presence and scowled at them.

They were suddenly returned to the lake where the disc was still fixed in mid-air. A blue light from the sky exploded against the back surface and the disc vanished instantly. Awestruck, they remained frozen in place and did not fully comprehend what they had just experienced. And then Jenny screamed and Ross jolted into action. "Let's get the hell out of here!"

Jenny was stiff as a statue until Ross shook her and snapped her out of it. "What did we just see?"

"I don't know. But we got to go." He darted towards the truck, jammed the key into the ignition and slammed the gas pedal down. The truck swerved across the dirt lot and the tires spun out rocks and dust. Hands tightly on the wheel, Ross sped down the highway as Jenny muttered incoherently.

"Are you okay, babe?"

"What did we just see?"

He wiped saliva off the side of his mouth. "Who knows? But it wasn't pretty."

She turned to him tearfully. "Where were we?"

"On some kind of ship, I guess. They were being tortured."

"What happened to the disc?"

They passed a few cars driving in the opposite direction. "No telling. It just blew up or something."

"Maybe we were just imaging it?"

"Both of us? No way."

"What are we going to do, Ross?"

"We got to tell your dad."

The late afternoon skyline faded red to purple over Jenny's huge two story house. Ross parked the truck in the driveway behind her mother's Lexus and Jenny ran towards the front door. "Mom, dad!" she shouted, rushing through the foyer and living room. Her mother saw that she was frightened. "What's the matter?" She held Jenny in place. "What's wrong?"

"Where's Daddy?"

Her father galloped down the staircase. "What's going on in here?"

"We have a problem, sir."

Jenny embraced her father and whimpered. "Daddy, it was a nightmare."

"What are you talking about?"

"We found something at the lake. It was from another world."

He held her out at arm's length. "Another world?"

"It's true, Mr. Carsdale. We found a gold disc at the lake and then I think we were taken off the planet. I know it sounds crazy, but it really happened."

"Daddy, he's telling the truth."

Mr. Carsdale glanced over at his bewildered wife. "All right. Let's go into the living room and talk this out. We need cooler heads."

"Sir, you know your daughter. She's level headed. And you know me. I'm not easily flustered. But we both saw something horrible."

"You kids aren't doing drugs, are you?"

Ross shook his head adamantly. "No way. I'm telling you this was real. We were on a space ship and these aliens were torturing other aliens. It was hard to watch."

Stunned, Mr. Carsdale's rubbed his jaw in a guarded fashion. "You haven't told anybody else about this?"

"No, Daddy."

"Good. Because if this gets out, the whole town will be talking. They'll think you're both insane."

"I don't care what they think, Mr. Carsdale."

"But I do. I don't want my family branded as those weird people down the street."

"This is serious, Dad."

He gestured to his wife. "Take Jenny upstairs and give her something to calm her down."

Ross nodded at her. "Go ahead, babe. I'll call you later."

Jenny followed her mother upstairs and Mr. Carsdale put his hand on Ross' shoulder. "I don't know what happened to you out there. It must be some kind of hallucination. I'm sure after a good night's sleep, you'll see things differently tomorrow."

"I know what we saw was real."

"I'm sure you think that. You'd better go home now."

Ross's father, unshaven and wearing torn blue jeans, was more trusting of his son's account. He had already finished off a bottle of whiskey and probably didn't care one way or the other. By midnight he had passed out on the sofa and Ross had gone up to his room and collapsed onto the bed. It was impossible for him to relax or sleep.

He blinked, opened his eyes wide and was back on board the alien vessel where the gray creatures maneuvered around a slender being with translucent skin. Ross stared at the helpless captive, who was missing eyes and ears, but had a small mouth left slightly agape. The creatures stood over the being and one of them carried a tray full of ominous tools.

Knowing what was coming next, Ross tried to interfere, but couldn't move. Another creature waved a red glowing wand over the captive's legs. They stepped backwards and the skin on its legs percolated, melted off the side of the table and fell onto the floor. The pain must have been excruciating because the being jerked its head up and down and thrashed about wildly.

After its legs had been dissolved, the creatures moved in for their next experiment. One of them held a knife like object and carved out the being's midsection. Another creature lifted the skin up and lowered a vacuum tube into its stomach and sucked out the contents.

Ross suddenly awoke on his mattress. Flinching from right to left, he was startled by his cell phone; which must have been buried somewhere in the folds of his quilt. He searched frantically and when he found it, Jenny was breathing heavily on the other end of the line. "It happened again!"

"Me too!"

"It was the same place."

"I know I wasn't asleep."

"I'm scared, Ross."

He sprung from the bed in a panic. "I'll be right there."

Ross grabbed his wallet, swiped the truck keys off the table and zipped past his unconscious father. A few blocks away from Jenny's house he parked the car next to a field and went on foot. His pace quickened when he thought he heard someone following him. He peered into the dark recesses behind the trees and bushes, fully expecting an ambush. Determining that his mind was playing tricks, he slipped around the side of Jenny's house and climbed up a familiar trellis.

Jenny met him at the window and solidly embraced him. "This is terrible. I can't take it much longer."

"I'm here now. You're safe."

"What are we going to do?"

"We got to think about our next move carefully. I don't know about you, but I'm not ending up on that table."

"Ross, we've got to tell the authorities about this. Of what I saw, these aliens are way more advanced than us."

"Yeah, but who do we tell? Your Dad's right about one thing. They'll probably think we're nuts."

"But we have to do something."

He glanced over at her desk top computer. "I got an idea. There's these UFO networks that deal with this kind of stuff."

"Let's do it."

Ross searched the web and found the name of a well know organization. "Here we are. C.U.F.O.R. The Center for Unidentified Flying Object Reports. Says here they'll send out a field interviewer within twenty-four hours."

"Perfect."

The next day Ross and Jenny were in his father's living room when there was a knock at the door. When Ross opened it, a man with thick rimmed glasses and a briefcase stood on the porch. "Ross Kellon?"

"Yes, come in. This is my girlfriend Jenny."

"You said this was urgent? Something about a gold disc."

"We've been seeing these awful experiments."

"What kind of experiments?"

Jenny almost cried. "Horrible Ones."

"You mentioned this happened at a lake?"

"Yeah, outside of town."

The investigator opened his briefcase and revealed two small electronic boxes. "I'd like to first go to that site and then later examine any articles you may have had that day."

"Just some fishing gear and food."

He seemed anxious. "Will you show me the event site? It's best to gather evidence closest to the encounter."

"Sure, let's go."

"We'll take my car." Ross sat in the passenger side, Jenny scooted into the back seat and they headed towards the lake. "This case was particularly interesting because we received a few other calls about unknown lights in this general area."

"Really?" Ross glanced back at Jenny. "Then we didn't imagine it."

"I'm not prepared to assume anything at this time. But there may be some unusual activity out here."

Ross directed him to the area at the lake where they had originally parked and lead him into the woods where he found the disc. He pointed over to a patch of ground. "It was sticking up right there."

The investigator removed an electronic device with a glass display screen. "This is an EMF detector."

"We know. We watch those ghost shows."

He bent over and the needle moved substantially. "This is odd."

"What?"

"I'm receiving a high EMF in this one location. I move away five feet or so, and it weakens."

"So something did happen."

"Can you tell me what occurred after you found the disc?"

Ross led him to the water's edge. "I brought it out here to show Jenny. It just flew out of my hands and stopped up in the air. And then a blue light—I mean a bright blue light exploded on the back of it."

The investigator surveyed other areas with the EMF detector, but the needle remained stationary. "There's nothing else. No unusual readings. But back there, it's a different story." He wiped some perspiration off his forehead. "I believe we can conclude this part of the investigation."

"So what do you think?"

He walked towards his car. "When you phoned us you mentioned that both of you experienced the same kind of visuals?"

"That's right."

The investigator rested his hand on the door latch. "Would you consider a session with a hypnotist?

"You think that will help?"

"It has proven beneficial in the past. If there's anything to these visions, it may help you to focus in on certain details."

Jenny interjected loudly. "We'll do it."

The interviewer nodded and drove them back to town.

When Jenny's father learned about the therapist's upcoming visit, he was livid. Jenny sat meekly on a living room chair as he paced from one end of the room to the other. "Of all the ridiculous things!"

Jenny's mother tried to pacify her husband. "Now Bill, what harm can this do? It may help clear up any doubts."

"Jenny hasn't had any visions in the past twenty four hours."

She rested her hand on his forearm. "But she's frightened that more will come. Let's do this for our daughter."

He begrudgingly complied. "All right, all right."

The sun was high overhead when the interviewer and the therapist arrived in the Carsdale driveway. Ross met them and helped bring in a video camera, tripod, several electronic devices and extension chords. Mr. Carsdale directed them to the living room, where the camera system would be erected. The therapist, an attractive woman in her early forties, set up a lap top computer on the end table between the couch and chair.

Mr. Carsdale wandered over to her. "You're a hypnotist?"

She smiled, and plugged in a power pack. "I use several methods. Hypnotism is just one of them."

"Umm . . ."

"Mr. Carsdale, you seem to have some apprehension?"

"I'm not much into that spooky stuff."

She nodded with familiarity. "I've heard that before. And it's not an entirely unreasonable position. Perhaps this will put your mind at ease. I'm a graduate of New York University and hold a degree in psychiatry."

"Impressive. So why this kind of work?"

"I often collaborate with paranormal investigators because I'm interested in the individual's state of mind when encountering these phenomena."

Ross brought Jenny into the living room. "This is my girlfriend."

"Hello, Jenny. My name is Dr. Virginia Baron. I'll be conducting the sessions."

"I want to go first."

"That's up to you."

The C.U.F.O.R. interviewer finished setting up the tripod and aimed the camera at the couch. "Good to go, doctor."

Dr. Baron gestured towards the couch. "Jenny, there's nothing to worry about. Have you ever been hypnotized before?"

"No."

"Nothing to it. Understand that you can't be hypnotized against your will. And once you're under I can't make you do anything you don't want to do."

"Just get me some answers."

"I hope I can help. I'll conduct the session in here. Everyone else will watch from the kitchen."

Ross squeezed Jenny's hand and ruffled her hair with assurance. "Sure you want to go first?"

"Now more than ever."

The interviewer strung cables into the kitchen and set up a laptop on the table. Ross and the Carsdale's pulled up chairs and scooted up close to him. "We'll record the session from here. This will give them privacy."

Dr. Baron sat on the chair next to Jenny. "I'll begin the process and you should be under in a matter of minutes."

Jenny expelled a lengthy breath. "I'm ready when you are."

Dr. Baron recited her hypnotic mantra and Jenny was now receptive. "I want to bring you back to the park where you saw the aliens."

"It was at the lake."

"Then at the lake. Who was there with you?"

"Ross. We were fishing."

"And then you and Ross saw something at the lake?"

"Ross found a gold disc."

"What happened after Ross found the disc?"

Jenny's face contorted. "It disappeared into a blue light."

"And then?"

"I can't see . . . I can't see." Jenny abruptly jolted off the couch, grabbed Dr. Baron's arm and leered at her with penetrating eyes. She tried to remove Jenny's hand, but was instantly transported to the alien laboratory. Unable to loosen her grip, Dr. Baron witnessed the same kind of mutilation that Jenny had seen in her visions.

The others in the kitchen were seemingly paralyzed as Dr. Baron's face twitched and her body spasmodically trembled. With one burst of strength, she yanked her arm away from Jenny and fell off the chair. Jenny returned to full consciousness and was disorientated and confused when she saw Dr. Baron on the floor. The others rushed in from the kitchen to help.

Speechless, Dr. Baron looked up at Jenny, leaped to her feet, bolted out the front door and ran down the sidewalk with the interviewer following closely behind. "I'll be back for my stuff." By the time he made it to the end of the driveway, she was almost at the intersection down the street.

Ross, Jenny and her parents waited on the front porch. Ross turned to Jenny. "What did you see?"

"I didn't see anything. I woke up and she was on the floor."

"That does it", Mr. Carsdale stated emphatically. "We're done."

Jenny held onto Ross. "She must have seen the aliens."

"But if she saw the aliens, why didn't we?"

Mr. Carsdale ushered them back into the house. "They'll be no more of this nonsense. Whether you believe this really happened to you or not, in two weeks you'll be taking your furniture up to the dorms and your mother and I are going to meet up there for the orientation. That's all we should be concerned with for now. This is the start of a new life for both of you. There's nothing more important than that. Don't complicate it by going on some stupid crusade."

The interviewer eventually returned alone to the Carsdale residence. Ross had already disassembled all the equipment and stacked it up by the front door. "Where's Dr. Baron?"

"She's pretty upset. She's not coming back. She claims she saw something that really frightened her."

"Then you believe us?"

"I don't know what to believe. I'm leaning towards classifying this case as a possible encounter. But this kind of investigation is way out of my league. I've notified my headquarters."

Mr. Carsdale forcefully stepped between them. "These kids have to go to college. You and your group can investigate some other time."

"You must admit that something unusual happened in that session."

"All I know is that some therapist freaked out. I didn't see any space people and my daughter doesn't remember anything about it."

Ross followed the interviewer out of the house. "Thanks for everything. I hope Dr. Baron's going to be okay."

"If anything happens again, please call me."

"This isn't going to be on some television show?"

"Our organization often guests on the UFO shows. We're not at that point yet. Still, word's going to get out."

A week had passed and Ross and Jenny had not seen any more visions. They were beginning to believe their ordeal was over and wearily settled into some kind of normalcy. They had made reservations for a rental truck and gathered a few friends to help pack their bulkiest items to transport to the dormitories. Jenny's mother, an ever diligent planner, made certain that her daughter would have everything she needed. She and her husband were booked on a flight to meet up with them a few days after they arrived at the college.

On Monday morning Ross, who had already loaded his table and desk into the truck, drove over to the Carsdale residence. Jenny looked forward to the change and couldn't wait to leave town. Her parents and a few high school friends had already set her belongings out in the yard and Ross helped them load up the truck.

Just before they departed, Mr. Carsdale embraced his daughter. "Now everything's going to be just fine."

"I hope so, Daddy."

"We'll be up there soon."

Her mother cradled her face with loving hands. "My baby's going to college."

"Don't worry, mom. Ross will look after me."

"I know he will."

Mr. Carsdale began to experience the loss a father feels for a departing daughter and gripped Ross' hand tightly. "Watch over her." Ross nodded, jumped up into the truck, started the motor and drove away from the house, leaving family and friends waving in the middle of the street. Though he felt uneasy passing the road to the lake, the six hour trip ahead gave him a sense of distance from all the bad memories.

"We're really moving away", Jenny exclaimed, looking ahead at the endless highway cutting between the open farmlands.

Ross patted the steering wheel. "And not soon enough."

She worriedly glanced over at him. "Are you second guessing everything that happened to us?"

"Not after what happened to Dr. Baron. But I do think if it was going to happen to us again, it would have already done so."

"There must have been some reason we received those visions."

"College is going to be a dud compared to what we've been through."

Jenny smiled. "At least there won't be any aliens."

They stopped for a snack at a roadside café, filled the gas tank and returned to the highway; which alternated from farmlands to higher altitude wooded areas. When they reached the city limits, Jenny did her best navigating Ross through a maze of unfamiliar roads. Soon the university grew out of a small neighborhood and they found their dormitories.

A flurry of students parked along the streets created a festive atmosphere where everyone helped each other unload furniture. Ross spotted some high school friends and enlisted their help. Jenny had just met her new roommate, who was arranging her desk and lamp against the wall. Once the move was completed, Ross and his friends caravanned over to the male dormitories and offloaded a batch of desks, tables and chairs.

The sun had just set and most of their possessions had already been removed. Ross had not met his roommate yet, but was expecting him the next day. He returned to Jenny and brought her back to his dormitory. Some of the students had already arranged an impromptu party, discretely smuggling in vodka and pouring it into a fruit punch. The moon was full that evening and the temperature had dropped to a balmy eighty degrees.

"We got the place alone tonight."

"I don't know what you have in mind, Ross Kellon. But you're not going to get me in trouble the first night we're here."

"Too bad. But to tell you the truth, I'm glad we're here and not at home." He turned away forlornly. "Still . . ."

"What's the matter? You look bummed."

"I was thinking about the lake. I just hope one day we can feel good about going back there."

She nuzzled up to him and put her arms around his waste. "As long as we have each other, I'm sure we'll go back one day."

"At least summer's a long way off."

They embraced firmly, kissed on the mouth and were transported in the blink of an eye back to the alien laboratory. Only this time there was something different. The lab was unoccupied and they were able to move about freely and converse with each other. She held onto him. "I can touch you. I can talk to you."

He held onto her hand. "I think we might really be here."

"Oh my God, then we're dead."

"Not if I can help it. I don't see any of them." He glanced over at the partially obscured central table. He tugged Jenny cautiously along with him and discovered a two foot long reptilian with yellow skin. Appearing unconscious and unharmed, it startled them when its multiple eyelids opened.

The reptilian communicated without moving its mouth. "You must get away from here."

"Who are you?"

"I come from the other side of the galaxy."

"How are you talking to us?"

"I am telepathic. You must leave now. As long as you are here on this vessel your lives are in danger."

"Who are we in danger from?"

"They are known as the Sargons. A hideous species. Malicious conquerors."

"Did they conquer you?"

"They will soon. You must leave while you have the capability to do so."

Ross pushed a mechanical arm out of the way. "Let me help you."

"It's too late for me. Save yourselves."

"We're not going without you."

The reptilian hissed at them. "You don't understand. The Sargons experiment on those they abduct in order to find weaknesses. My planet is doomed. You can still get away."

"But we're here now. How can we get away?"

"No, you are still on your planet. You must have found the disc."

Jenny nodded. "We did."

The reptilian lifted his head. "That's how they take you. They follow the disc. They must have already discovered your planet and its people."

"Then what can we do?"

"Escape as far away from where you found the disc."

The door slid open and three of the gray creatures scampered into the laboratory. Ross tucked Jenny behind him and prepared for the worst. The creatures seem to detect their presence and moved rapidly towards them. Ross did his best to shelter Jenny against a bulkhead.

In a flash Jenny pulled away from their kiss in the dormitory room. "What just happened?"

Ross nervously juggled the keys in his pocket. "We got to go."

"But to where?"

"You heard. As far away as we can."

"But what about our parents?

"Forget about them. They can't help us. The Sargons are coming"

"But where can we go?"

"I don't know. Anywhere but here."

They dashed out of the room, left the door open, leaped into the truck and sped away from the campus. Ross accelerated down the highway under a full moon that shined over the hills like frosting on a cake. As they traveled further away from the city, there were numerous stars in the night sky.

One hour after they left the university, Ross became increasingly concerned about Jenny, who was silent with her head pressed against the passenger window. "What you thinking about, babe?"

She straightened out. "We were so happy."

"We'll be happy again."

"We had so many plans; so many dreams. You were going to be a business major, play for the team. I was getting my sociology degree." She barely grinned. "I even thought we might start a family one day."

"We still can. We're not done yet."

"If what that poor alien said was true, the Sargons are going to arrive soon. Funny thing, everybody's going about their lives, thinking nothing's going to happen. We're the only two people that know the truth."

"Let's hope we can get away and warn the military."

Jenny gazed out the front windshield. "Here we are running for our lives and all I can think about is how beautiful and peaceful all those stars are." She tilted her head curiously. "What's that?

"What?"

"That star. It's brighter than the others."

Alternately watching the road and the sky, he studied the star. "Maybe it's Venus." He released his foot from the gas pedal. "Or maybe not."

Jenny began to breathe heavily. "Ross?"

He turned onto the embankment. "Let's wait a minute."

She peered out the passenger window at a dense wall of trees and bushes; and then looked back out the windshield. "You think it's them?"

"I don't know. It's not changing, or anything."

The light suddenly grew larger and Ross ordered her to get the flashlight from the glove compartment and leave the truck. As he rounded the front grill, the light grew at a much faster pace.

"Ross, I'm scared."

"I know. Let's get out of here."

She handed him the flashlight, he shined it on the trees and located a marginal opening through the foliage. They crunched twigs and leaves beneath their shoes, forging a new path where none had been before. Jenny clutched onto his shirt tail, pointed at the truck now visible though a narrow clearing in the brush and same blue light they had seen at the lake enveloped it. As delicately and quietly as possible, Ross pulled her deeper into the woods.

They trudged headlong into the darkness and the road and the truck had disappeared from view. Jenny came upon what she believed was a well defined path, which hastened their escape. "Do you think we made it?"

"Keep moving."

They climbed steadily to the top of a low ridge where they could better examine the terrain. Spotting a gully at the bottom of the hill, Ross yanked her by the hand down the rocky surfaces. Once in the gully, Jenny thought she saw something out of the corner of her eye.

"Ross, wait!"

"What's the matter?"

"I guess it was nothing."

A blue light flashed against some trees and then ducked into the bushes on the other side of the gully. They crouched down and remained motionless as the blue light, now resembling a five foot orb, darted out from the trees, floated along the middle of the gully and then retreated back into the woods. "It's looking for us", she whispered.

"I think we lost it."

They crept in the opposite direction of the orb and thought they were free. Moments later it appeared in the path ahead of them. Ross dropped the flashlight, held onto Jenny and they ran in the opposite direction; tripping over rocks and tree branches until rolling down the other side of a hill. Battered and confused, they laid flat on their stomachs. "Don't move."

"I don't hear anything."

"That's just it. No insects. No nothing."

A flicker of light pieced the shadowy foliage above them. They held onto each other as the light spilled over the ridge and lit them up on every side. There was a blinding flash of white light and they were instantly transported to a cramped metallic room with slightly vibrating surfaces and a solitary bench where Jenny curled up in the corner.

Ross tested every surface with his finger tips. "They got us. We must be on their ship. Looks like there's only one door in here."

"So it's over."

"I'm not giving up that easy."

But what can we do? You saw what happened to the others."

"I'm not going to let anything happen to you."

She sighed helplessly. "We tried, Ross. We never had a chance."

Ross turned his head when he heard something on the other side of the door. He pressed his ear against the metal surface and detected muted scuffling noises and what he thought were voices. He backed away and joined her on the bench and the door slid open.

Expecting the worse, they were relieved when a friendly old man with white hair entered the room. Ross peeked behind the man to see if the little gray creatures were following closely behind. "Who are you?"

"I have taken this form in order to converse with your species. I apologize for the ordeal you have suffered."

"Apologize? Why are you doing these medical experiments?"

He smiled assuredly. "There are no medical experiments here. There never were. The malevolent aliens never existed."

Ross stood to his feet. "I don't understand."

"In a way you were part of an experiment. But you need not concern yourselves any longer."

Infuriated, Jenny stood up. "How can you say that? You put us through hell."

"Believe me, it was necessary."

"Why?"

"That's difficult to explain. You will not remember any of this, because none of this actually happened."

"But we found the disc."

"There never was a disc. There never were any Sargons. You are a decent species and deserve a chance to survive. We will return you now."

Hundreds of miles above the Earth's atmosphere, two spheres of pure energy communicated with each other. "Then we are in agreement?"

"This is a promising race. They have a right to prosper."

"Then you will present a favorable report?"

"It is obvious they are too vulnerable to defend themselves."

"I concur. Any species with telepathic abilities could easily manipulate them. They will need protection. We shall order a system wide quarantine."

Ross and Jenny reclined on a blanket under a shade tree and kept vigil over their fishing poles stuck into the clay soil at the water's edge. The summer days at the lake were coming to an end and the rigors of college would soon occupy their lives. They were in love and would nourish their relationship well beyond the confines of their sheltered town. Jenny cuddled up safely within her lover's arms and chest, poking her toes between his. It was still humid and there were only a few clouds high above the lake.

"That's funny."

"What?"

"That cloud over there."

"What about it?"

"It looks like a sailor with a beard."

He stared oddly. "That's what it looks like to you?"

"Yeah. Not you?"

"Looks more like a bowl."

"Ross, you have no imagination. It's an old sailor. And you know what?" She caressed his face. "He's watching over us."

"Now that's really dumb."

BAKERY

The elite military squad wearing dark garments covering green scaly skin surrounded a metal and glass building in the merchant's district. They awaited orders, sliding their reptilian tongues across rows of sharp teeth and then occasionally licking their bulbous eyeballs. Several aerial vehicles passed over the neighborhood as curious citizens flocked behind temporary barriers.

The squad's lead officer gave the orders to attack the occupants and with disciplined precision they crashed through the front and rear doors. Weapon's drawn; they discovered the shop was completely abandoned. The lead officer called into headquarters. "Site has been breached."

"Casualties?"

"None, sir."

There was a momentary pause. "Sorry. I didn't get that."

"There's nobody here. It's empty. Everything's gone."

"That's impossible. We verified their presence minutes ago. They couldn't have escaped."

"I repeat, targets are not present. No explanation."

"Not good enough. They were serving customers all day. They had no time to clear out."

"Sir, I know this sounds unbelievable, but this establishment appears to have been abandoned for a long time. I'm calling in a forensics team."

"Very well, resume your search. Report back to us if anything changes."

"Affirmative."

Hundreds of light years away a planet with tall, hairless beings with blue skin went about their daily lives with the vigor and enthusiasm of any technologically advanced society. They had strong leaders, a booming economy and a powerful military. In one of the numerous shops in the merchant's district, slender blue fingers dipped into a bowl and withdrew a thick glob of sweet batter. "This mixture is absolutely divine. Just the right amount of ingredients."

"You should be the envy of the galaxy."

"Yes, if things were different." He surveyed the rows of empty shelves. "By tomorrow morning, I shall fill this store with delicious treats that will beckon the most skeptical of pallets."

"As you always do."

"Very well. Let's get on with it."

In one particular suburb where colorful facades and rounded corners were the preferred architecture, Chal, his wife Tib and their daughter and son lived comfortably in a mushroom shaped house with a yard full of turquoise and yellow flowers. Bald as any male of the species, Tib and her daughter Mlaki brought the evening's dinner plates into the kitchen after a sumptuous meal. Chal and his son

Rol waited anxiously as Tib returned with a tray full of unfamiliar, yet hypnotically fragrant desserts of all shapes and sizes.

"Where did you get these", asked Chal? He reached out and grabbed a small square cake.

"A new bakery down the street."

"Oh yes. I passed it on the way home from work yesterday."

Mlaki brought out another plate with different kinds of desserts. "Sorry Rol. These are for you."

Dejected, Rol tried to be brave. "Wish I could eat those other ones."

Tib comforted her son with a slender palm across his cheek. "I know it's difficult, but you're allergic."

"But they look so good."

Chal tasted one. "These are delicious."

Tib shot him a stern glance. "I'm sure they're not that good."

"Yes, my dear. They're just all right."

Rol smiled at his father. "It's okay, dad. It's not your fault I can't digest that stuff. Go ahead and enjoy your cakes."

Mlaki eagerly consumed a dessert bar. "These are incredible. I've never tasted anything like them." She looked over at her brother. "Sorry Rol."

Chal selected another piece, but then drew his hand back. "I think I've had enough for now. Everything in moderation."

Mlaki refrained from taking another cake herself. "You're right, dad. I'll have some tomorrow."

As soon as Tib brought the desserts back into the kitchen, she snatched one of the squares off the tray and devoured it. Mlaki entered soon after and removed another square and jammed it into her pocket. An hour later, Chal wandered into the kitchen and shoved the last remaining cake into his mouth just as his son entered.

"Hey dad."

Chal's mouth bulged with a partially chewed cake and he immediately turned around and poured a glass of orange milk. Barely able to speak, he washed down the last morsel. "Hello, son."

"You promised we'd play Tigori 6."

"Select the level and let's do it."

Word quickly spread about the new bakery nestled between a toy store and a flower mart. A line of patrons formed early in the morning and the proprietor, who was also the chief baker, became familiar with his customer's daily orders. They presented a variety of exotic fare that would disappear as fast as it was placed on the shelves. Thanks to the restocking efforts of the proprietor and his assistant, finances were swiftly transacted, bags were filled with treats and customers were barely out the door before gobbling up their purchases.

The baker weighed a dozen cakes. "These are the ones with jelly in them."

"They're my favorites."

"They're a little more expensive."

"I don't care what they cost."

The proprietor smiled. "It pleases me you're satisfied."

"You should open up these shops throughout the solar system."

He wrapped up the cakes. "We intend to expand."

"I'll be back tomorrow."

After waiting an hour, Chal finally stepped up to the front of the line. Though feeling a tinge of guilt, he couldn't resist the lure of the cake squares. He devoured them in successive bites on his way to work, stabbing at the crumbs that fell on his pants. He knew he could never bring them home because of his son's digestive intolerance.

A few hours later it was Tib who stood in a line that stretched half way around the block. She recognized some of her neighbors, who all had guilty expressions as if they were hiding secrets. Some of the customers whispered about their favorite cakes, but most remained silent. Tib was only three customers away from the counter when the crowd became impatient with an elderly male who couldn't make a decision. In a matter of minutes the other customers harassed him enough to move the line again.

Tib was then greeted by the proprietor. "Can I help you?"

"Yes. I'll take those squiggly bars with the syrup on top."

"Indeed." He winked at her. "They're my favorites, too."

"I'll take three."

"Can I interest you in these jellies?"

She glanced around the shop as if expecting to see a member of her family or one of her closest friends. "I don't think so. These should be enough."

"Probably just the right amount."

"I think your bakery is marvelous. Pretty soon the line will go on for blocks."

He leaned in towards her. "I'll give you a hint. If you come right before sunrise, the line isn't so bad."

"I'll remember that."

"Here you are. Enjoy."

The children's voices echoed off nearby buildings in the school playground as Rol sat down with five of his closest friends. When the conversation turned to the new bakery, he felt disenfranchised. "I don't see what the big deal is."

One of his friends mocked him. "Course you wouldn't. All you can eat is that green mushy stuff."

"I can eat more than that. I have special desserts."

"I tasted one, remember. It tasted like dirt."

"No it doesn't!"

"Yes it did, you jerk."

Another friend appeared to sympathize with him. "Quit picking on Rol. He can't help it if he has to eat dirt."

"Shut up!"

"My mom gives us plenty of those cakes every night. I guess my mom's nicer than yours, Rol."

He started to walk away. "I'm not listening to this stupid nonsense anymore."

Another one of them laughed. "You're just jealous."

"Rol's a cry baby, Rol's a cry baby." They all chanted simultaneously.

"You know I get sick if I eat that stuff."

"Let's leave the cry baby alone."

When Chal's work day ended, he couldn't resist stopping by the bakery for one last cake square. The line was long as usual and he knew he would miss dinner if he stayed. Though conflicted, he decided to wait and purchase the cakes. Two hours later he paid for them and on the way out of the shop he consumed them with as much gratification as one could receive from any pleasure. As far as he was concerned, nothing was better; and if that meant disappointing his family, so be it.

Tib angrily greeted her husband in the living room. "Where have you been? This is the third night you've been late."

"I've been at work."

"Every night?"

Chal snapped at her. "If I have to work late, I have to work late."

Rol and Mlaki, seated at the living room table doing their homework, were surprised to see their parents arguing. Tib stood up and went nose to nose with her husband. "Don't speak to me that way!"

"What about you? You disappear every morning before getting our breakfast."

She was somewhat disarmed. "I've . . . been exercising."

"At our expense?"

Mlaki intervened. "Come on, you two. Get along."

He glared at his daughter contemptuously. "This is none of your business."

"But daddy, this is futile."

"Keep it up and I'll take a strap to you."

Disgusted, Mlaki ran up to her bedroom.

Tib turned around and stomped towards the kitchen. "Perhaps she needs a good whipping. She's been awfully mouthy to me lately."

Rol pleaded with his parents. "Mlaki didn't do anything. And you never hit us before."

Chal slowly nodded. "You're right, Rol. I don't know what I was thinking."

Mlaki locked her bedroom door, rummaged through her dresser, pulled out a box of jelly filled cakes and gorged herself while lying on her bed. She finished the entire contents of the box without the least bit concern for her girlish figure. She even refused a male friend's invitation to a party in order to plot her next trip to the bakery.

The next morning Tib had left the house early and stood in line as she had done every morning. She met a few neighbors, who among other things complained that some customers were holding places for their friends. When a heated dispute threatened violence, the proprietor's assistant stepped between the raucous offenders. "Please, no fighting. There's plenty to go around."

"They shouldn't be able to save places."

"You are correct. And we will not serve them."

A few offending customers grumbled, but soon relented when faced with a denial of service. Tib rested her elbows on the counter, ordered two bags of cakes and waited for her children to leave for school before returning home. She paraded around the house in ecstasy, stuffing the square cakes in her mouth and then collapsing on the sofa.

At school Rol noticed that his friends were behaving erratically. He couldn't understand what was troubling them, only that they were impatient and contemptible. Like most children they often teased each other and occasionally fought; but now the best of friends threatened each other with bodily harm. Rol didn't understand why these things were happening; only that he didn't want to be around them anymore.

Even in class his teacher acted differently. She used to be friendly and helpful, but now ridiculed many of them for making simple mistakes. After class, Rol inquired about his most recent test. "Excuse me, but can I have a word with you?"

"What is it?"

"I missed two questions and you said you were disappointed in me."

"I was disappointed."

"The note said that I was stupid."

She rested both hands on her hips. "You were stupid for making those mistakes. What kind of idiot would make such mistakes? This conversation is over."

"But?"

"That's all, Rol. You can go now."

Things weren't any easier at home where Rol found his mother and sister endlessly bickering. He tried to intervene, but they pushed him aside. Finally Mlaki had enough and charged out of the house, vowing she'd never return. Extremely upset, Rol had never seen his family in such turmoil. His mother and sister had always been so close and rarely disagreed about anything.

Chal stood in line at the bakery for over two hours. Tempers continued to flare as customers pushed and shoved one another to protect their space. Chal even sniped at work acquaintances that were eager to sink their teeth into the delicious desserts. When he arrived at the counter, the proprietor knew exactly what he wanted and filled his bag while complimenting him on his selection.

Rol hadn't seen his sister in a few days. She quietly knocked on his bedroom door, put her hand over his mouth and told him to listen. "I don't want mom and dad to know I'm here."

"What's the matter? Where did you go?"

"Quit asking so many questions. I stayed at a friend's house. Anyway, I'm grounded for a month."

"Mom was really mad at you."

"You don't know the half of it. Look at what she did to me." Mlaki turned around and dropped her shirt to reveal severe bruising.

"She's never hit you before."

"Just shut up and listen. I need you to go by the bakery early in the morning and buy me some cakes. I can't get away. They're even watching me at school."

"What is with that bakery?"

"Just do what I say."

"I'll go before school. Did you tell dad what mom did to you?"

"He told me I'd better straighten up, or he'd do worse."

"What's happening to us? Everything's weird now. We never had these kinds of fights before."

She scowled at him. "Never mind, Rol. Just get me the cakes. Let me worry about the parents."

Rol went to bed that night and tried to understand why his family life was deteriorating before his eyes. In the morning, he got up extra early and snuck out of the house. It was still dark, but when he rounded the corner there was already a long line at the bakery. He was about to take his place when he noticed his mother near the front entrance. He quickly ducked around the building and waited for her to purchase her goods. When she was gone, he rejoined the line.

That day at school Rol could only think about seeing his mother at the bakery. She had been telling her family she was exercising, but now he knew she was lying. He had always trusted his mother and he contemplated if he should inform his father. Between the unexplainable vitriol at home and his fellow students preferring confectionary over lunch every day, Rol began to suspect that the bakery was responsible for all these aberrations.

When he arrived home from school, he confronted his mother while she in the kitchen with her favorite sweets. "Oh, Rol, I didn't see you."

"Hi mom. Can I ask you something?"

"Yes, of course."

"I saw you at the bakery this morning."

"Oh, you did. Yes. I was there."

"Is that where you've been going every morning?"

"Not every morning. You're not going to tell your father?"

He looked down shyly. "If you don't want me to."

"Let's keep this our little secret." She cocked her head. "By the way, why were you there? You can't eat that stuff."

"I'd rather not say."

"Fair enough. You keep my secret, I won't ask yours."

A few hours later Chal arrived home late from work again. Tib was furious with him and they argued near the foyer. "Every night you've been coming home late."

"That's my business. You're just the wife."

"Oh, just the wife, huh? You're having an affair. I know it."

"Don't be ridiculous."

"I hate you. You're nothing but a liar."

"I hate this family."

Tib abruptly departed, and then turned around. "Take your stupid daughter and son away and leave me alone."

"Oh, you'd like that. Leave the brats with me. Why can't you take them?"

Rol boldly stood between his parents. "Look at you two. You never acted this way before. You love each other."

Chal gazed down at his son with dispassionate eyes. "You're nothing to me. You've caused us nothing but trouble."

He glanced over at his mother. "Is that true, mom?"

"Just go to your room. We've already arranged for you and sister to attend a boarding school." Rol dashed off to his bedroom and cried as his parents fought well into the night. Although Mlaki had previously heard about the boarding school, her immediate concern was that the school wasn't located within the vicinity of the bakery. Rol spent a sleepless night trying to figure out what to do next.

In the morning Tib left early to the bakery and Rol later purchased cakes for his sister. Only this time he didn't go right home. He stopped at the police station where an officer greeted him. "What is it kid? You look like you got something on your mind."

Rol seemed flustered and was unable to answer.

"Come on, come on, I haven't got all day." He stared menacingly at him.

"There's something happening at the bakery."

"The one down the street?"

"Yes, that's the one."

"They haven't closed, have they?"

Rol tilted his head curiously. "Not that I know of. But there's something evil going on there."

"Is that all? I thought something was really wrong."

"You don't understand, officer. Something is really wrong. People are acting real strange."

"In what way?"

"Like the bakery is all that matters."

He laughed. "You're just imagining things, kid."

"It's affecting my family. Everybody's mad at each other."

"Don't worry. We'll take a look."

"Thanks."

Rol walked away and the officer pulled out a bag of cakes and swallowed them voraciously as if it were his last meal.

After making the delivery to his sister, Rol went to school while most of his friends had stayed home. His teacher, who was still hostile, barely taught any subject that day and was preoccupied by the cookies hidden in her desk drawer. When the final bell rang, Rol went to the park across the street from the bakery and waited for his father to take his place at the end of the line. Still hidden behind a tree, he joined his father just before he reached the counter. "What are you doing here, son?"

"I just wanted to be with you."

His father seemed oblivious. "I guess it's all right. But I'm not changing my mind about the boarding school."

"I know, dad."

"You kids have been such a burden to us. You never use to be that way."

"You're right. We deserve it."

"They'll teach you some manners."

"I'm going to check out the cakes."

Intent on keeping his space in line, Chal didn't notice that Rol had wandered out of his sight. The baker and his customers were so busy dispensing and receiving goods that Rol was able to slip behind the counter, duck into a short hallway and hide in a broom closet behind a shelf of cleaning supplies. When the last customer had been served, the proprietor and his assistant locked up the premises.

"Sold more than yesterday. It keeps getting better."

The assistant began to communicate in an unknown foreign language.

"Speak in their tongue. I don't want you giving us away like you did last time."

"I apologize. It won't happen again.

The proprietor snickered deviously. "But you are correct about one thing. I am quite the artist."

"When it comes to baking, you have no competition."

"We can remain here for a long time if we're careful."

The assistant moved towards the closet, opened the door and Rol stiffened his back against the wall. "I'm going to clean up."

The proprietor shut the door. "Do that later. I'm weak. I need energy."

"As you wish."

Rol was able to breathe again and waited for them to retreat into the back room. He opened the closet door and heard some kind of humming noise. He gingerly crept along the wall and approached the slightly opened door to the back room. He peeked inside and saw a partially obscured glowing object behind a table cluttered with pots and pans. He crawled quietly to get a better view and stopped just short of the edge of the table.

Two strange dwarfs with rubbery layers of folded skin leaned over a circular metallic object with a glowing light. The odd creatures seem to be spreading their hands over the light, reeling back and forth in ecstasy as the machine continued to emit the low humming sound.

Speculating that the creatures were the baker and his assistant, Rol was frightened and unsure of what to do next. He tried to back away and then toppled over a long handled spatula resting against the side of the table. He froze and they suddenly turned around. "Who's there?"

The creatures circled around the table from opposite directions. "So what do we have here?"

Rol stood up. "Nobody. I wasn't doing anything."

"A curious boy."

"He's seen us, Joran."

"Yes, he has."

"I won't tell. I promise."

Their faces were as wrinkled as their bodies. "Oh, we'll make certain of that. Does my appearance disturb you?"

"What are you?"

"As you've probably guessed, we're not from around here."

Rol pointed at the humming light. "What's that?"

"This device filters and prepares our food. We use it to drain the life source from others. We consume their energy."

"So you're parasites?"

"Ahh, you pay attention in your science studies. The sweets I bake have a substance that extracts nourishment from the host species. When one of your kind consumes our desserts and returns for more, the machine does its work very efficiently. Unfortunately one of the side effects is a personality alteration. We've tried to prevent that sort of thing over the years; but haven't had much success."

"I'm going to stop you."

He laughed. "Who will you go to? Who would believe you?"

The assistant began moving around the table. "This one's different. He hasn't been affected. But why?"

"I'm allergic."

The baker closed his eyes. "That explains everything. You were in earlier with your father. I must sadly report that you have lost him and your family forever. There are no reversals for the victims."

Rol spotted a metallic tube resting on top of the table. "I'm going to stop you."

"No, we are going to stop you."

Rol grabbed the pipe, lifted it over his head and smashed it down on the humming light, causing sparks to explode and sending the aliens into a panic. As the proprietor raced over to shut it off, he ordered the assistant to seize Rol; who nimbly dodged his swooping arm and ran around the table as the machine fizzled to abrupt halt.

"Get him!"

He ran past the closet and into the main shop, where the assistant chased him between the aisles. The proprietor joined in the pursuit and they almost cornered him when Rol tipped a shelf over that almost buried them. The assistant put a hand on him, but Rol was able to push over another shelf that crashed through the window. Without hesitation, he leaped over the splinters of broken glass and out onto the street. Just as the assistant was about to pursue him, the proprietor held him back.

"Never mind. Let him go."

"What about the inducer?"

"It's damaged. We'll have to repair it."

"And the boy?"

The proprietor gazed around the shop. "I'm afraid our stay here on this world has come to an end."

"But it was so promising."

"We can't take the chance someone may believe the boy. It's best to pack up and leave."

He head bowed. "I'll prepare the transference cycle."

It was a cool early morning in the Spanish city of Granada where beautiful buildings were set against a wall of high mountains. A few businesses were already in full production, but for the most part the streets were abandoned and the citizens were still asleep. As the hours passed by and the sunlight began to spread across the city proper, two female students from the college were exploring their newly adopted home.

"Maria, look down there."

"What?"

"It's a chocolate store."

"Is it open?"

"Let's take a look."

The women strolled into the shop and the proprietor, a balding man with a mustache was pushing candy trays into the glass cabinets by the register. He glanced over at them and smiled. "Good morning. Can I interest you in a sample?"

"Sure."

He selected two chocolate drips and placed them in wrappers. When they bit into the chocolate, they swooned and their eyes fell back into their heads. "These are incredible. Absolutely wonderful."

"It pleases me that you find them so delectable."

The other girl finished her treat. "I've never had anything this good."

"Tell your friends we're open for business."

"You can count on that."

The baker smiled deviously. "I have no doubt."

GIRLFRIEND

David Brand's loft apartment started out clean, but ended up messy. The young scientist had access to the most sophisticated equipment at his Cal Tech laboratory, yet his home was littered with computers, processors, expensive software and electronic toys. He had little time to pick up after himself, but had the sense to keep the refrigerator stocked and the kitchen counters free. As for the rest of the apartment, the floors and tables were covered with boxes, magazines and discarded monitor screens.

David often huddled next to his upgraded systems and entered precise calculations well into the night. Even on the weekends he buried himself in a cloistered world of numbers and figures. On this day he expected a visit from his mother, who let herself in with a key and was abruptly halted when the door hit something. "I'm stuck!"

Eye's sore from gazing too long at the screen; he maneuvered around several boxes and spotted his mother's face peeking through the door jamb. "What's wrong? Come on in."

"Something's blocking me."

He slid a box away from the door. "Okay, all clear."

She carried a bag of groceries. "Your place is a death trap."

"You say that every time."

"It's just not healthy to live this way."

"I'm working. What else can I tell you?"

"I brought you something to eat."

He took the bag from her and set it on the kitchen counter. Thanks, mom. Sit down and relax."

"Thank God there's a place to sit."

"Want something to drink?"

"I'll have coffee."

He heated up the water in the microwave. "How's your card tournaments?"

"I've been winning more than losing." She watched him dip a coffee bag in the steaming cup. "So, any girls I should know about?"

"Mother."

"It's just that your sisters are happily married."

"Ed's a truck driver and Dick's at the post office."

"They've given me three grandchildren."

"When have I heard that before?"

"It's not normal to be cooped up in here all the time."

"Mom, I'm analyzing significant data."

She sipped her coffee. "What happened to that earthquake girl?"

"Scientist. She was a scientist. And we had a few dates. It didn't work out."

"And that slug girl?"

Frustrated, he closed his eyes. "She studied snails. But to be honest, she always smelled like formaldehyde."

"I just don't want you to end up some lonely mad scientist."

"I'll try to avoid that fate."

David's department at the California Institute of Technology was a bastion of theoretical physics and quantum mechanics. The head professor was Charles Maydon, a well respected scientist in his own right. David was no doubt his most promising subordinate, even though at times he felt his methods overshadowed common sense. He scanned David's monitor screen. "Paradox?"

"Close, yet so far."

He chuckled. "Everyone's far from the unified theory." He patted his shoulder. "The holy grail of all things doesn't come easy."

"It boils down to the math, Charles. And that's absolute and unforgiving."

"I'm the last one to discourage your work. It would mean a great deal to science. And you've certainly progressed further than most. My only fear is that these grand schemes often elude us."

"True. Most say the unified theory is out of reach."

"On the other hand, how many changes have you seen in cosmology in your lifetime? New discoveries seem to upend our previous concepts on a regular basis."

"Those are the quirks of quarks."

He smiled. "Particle physics is an open science. All I can do is encourage you to persevere." He walked away, and then spun around. "Oh, you are attending the party tomorrow evening?"

He winced. "I guess so."

"Good. Remember that public relations can be a scientist's best friend."

"How can I forget? You keep reminding me."

David rummaged through his apartment and picked out a sports coat, pants and a tie with a small stain across one of its diagonal stripes. He brushed his teeth, combed his hair and shined his best shoes with a damp rag. He drove to the hotel where the college had reserved a banquet room for the department chiefs and their important donors. While most sipped champagne and selected a variety of hors d'oeuvres, David tried his best to indulge the wealthy donors with scientific banter.

As the evening progressed, David looked for signs he might be able to slip away. Across the room he noticed a beautiful young woman with brown wavy hair, deep green eyes and white teeth approach him with champagne glasses. As the guests plucked the glasses off her tray, he ogled her frilly serving outfit and tight fitting shorts. Infatuated, he watched her move closer towards him. As she was about to extend her tray, she tripped, spilled the last remaining glassful on him and frantically dabbed his coat with a small towel. "I'm sorry. I'm so sorry."

"It's okay. No harm done."

"I'm such a klutz."

"No, it's really okay. Most of it missed me."

Though only a few guests even realized what had happened, she nervously surveyed the room. "It's the third time I've done this. If my boss finds out, I'm fired."

David gestured for her to follow him outside. "We won't let him find out."

"She. My boss is a she."

"Either way, you're in the clear."

"Thanks. You're so nice."

"So are you. What's your name?"

"Lesa Martin."

"I'm David Brand."

She held out her hand to shake his. "Nice to meet you, David. Be honest, I shouldn't be doing this kind of work."

"We all have our moments."

"So, you're some kind of scientist?"

"A physicist."

She cocked her head. "Sound's important."

"So what do you do when you're not serving drinks?"

"I'm an actress. Not a very good one. That's why I'm doing the catering work."

"An actress, ehh? Well you certainly have the look for it." He wondered if he was too forward. "I mean . . . you look perfect. I mean . . ."

"Thanks, David. That's sweet." She hesitated. "Maybe I'm being too bold, but would you like to go out and have dinner with me some time?"

"You want to go out with me? Sure."

"Do you have a number?"

He reached in his wallet. "I keep these fancy embossed cards for these kinds of events."

"I'll call you soon."

She turned around and disappeared into the crowded banquet room. Never in his wildest dreams did he ever think a woman like Lesa would ask him out on a date. Unable to concentrate on anything else, he found it difficult to associate with any of the donors or even his colleagues for the rest of the evening.

Lesa arranged to meet David at the kind of trendy restaurant that he rarely frequented. He realized that his clothes were outdated and asked one of his sisters to help him purchase something appropriate for the date. He entered the restaurant in a new vest, silk shirt, loose tie and casual shoes. Lesa waved to him from a table and greeted him with a quick peck on the cheek.

"David, you look great."

"Thanks. You look gorgeous."

"Hunrgy?"

"A little."

The restaurant was packed with wardrobe conscious youth and a loud playing sound system. David tried to portray a veneer of confidence by forming his sentences in his mind before blurting out any awkward statements. After twenty minutes of small talk it was obvious that Lesa had put him at ease with her natural charms.

"So what you do?"

"I'm a research scientist at Cal Tech."

"You must be really smart. I'm dumb when it comes to science and history and other smart things like that."

"I mostly study the universe for a living."

"Like the stars? I always wanted to go to Venus. It's such a romantic place."

"Actually, Venus is kind of hot. Not very hospitable."

"Really? I thought there were flowers and plants."

"It's much closer to the sun than the Earth."

She sighed. "I told you I wasn't very smart. And when it comes to math, I'm really lost."

"You have other attributes. You're very down to earth."

"You mean close to the ground?"

"See, you have a good sense of humor." They ordered parfait drinks with crooked straws. "Now it's your turn to tell me about you, Lesa."

"Not much to my story."

"Come on, you're a beautiful girl and an actress."

"A 'wanna be' actress." She shrugged and tilted her head. "Okay, I might as well tell you all the gory details. I just got out of a three year relationship with a successful producer. I'm kind of messed up now. I'm not sure what to do next. That's why I'm working in catering."

"Was the boyfriend thing a mutual decision?"

"He promised me acting jobs. And in all honestly he did open doors for me. I guess I just wasn't that good of an actress. But I knew it was over when I found him cheating on me. It's an old story. Typical Midwest girl heads to Hollywood and ends up damaged goods."

"You're not damaged. You just had a bad relationship. But his loss is my gain. I really like you." He sighed. "Look at me. I'm trying to find a mathematical solution to something that probably doesn't have one."

"So, what's this math problem? Like I told you before, I'm terrible at math."

"A unified theory. The answer to everything."

"Wow. That's big."

"I'm no closer than when I started out five years ago."

"You'll figure it out. For now, let's eat. I'm starved."

When the meal arrived they were cognoscente of every mouthful of food. After several minutes they were relaxed enough to allow some bits of food to occasionally appear in their mouths during conversations. Lesa confided that she never received a grade higher than a 'C' and David alluded to his inexperience dating women. After dinner, he followed her in his car and walked up to her apartment door.

"I had a great time, David."

"Me too."

She paused, then took the initiative and kissed him on the lips. "I'd like to go out with you again, if that's okay?"

"Yes. Yes. That would be great."

She removed a piece of paper from her purse and scribbled her phone number on it. "Call me."

Lesa opened her front door, slipped inside and David giddily shuffled back to his car. He couldn't believe that a simple beverage spill from a waitress would change his life. The following day he hired a five person cleaning crew and oversaw the disposal of half the accumulated junk in his apartment. Eight hours later he couldn't recognize the place.

Stomach fluttering, he picked up the phone and entered Lesa'a number. "Hi, it's David."

"You called. I'm so happy."

"Anyway, I was thinking we could . . . we could . . . go out to dinner and a movie next week?"

"Sure, I'd love to. But why do we have to wait? What are you doing tonight?"

"Nothing. Well, just some work. But nothing."

Cool. Where should we go?"

"I know this good Japanese restaurant."

"I love sashimi. Pick me up in an hour"

They sat at the bar and watched the chef prepare dozens of sumptuous appetizers. Fortunately for David, Lesa had the uncanny ability to keep the conversation flowing throughout his most awkward silences. She fed him a piece of tuna, and then laughed as a morsel slid down the side of his mouth. "So my mother tells me, Hollywood's not the place for me. And my father grounds me until I'm twenty-one. But they knew I was determined to go and in the end supported me all the way."

"Your parents sound reasonable."

"They're terrific. I think down deep they knew if I stayed I'd end of serving fast food all my life."

"You're too hard on yourself."

"That's easy for you to say. You're a genius. You know all kind of subjects."

"We just have different interests when it comes to academia. You run with the Hollywood set and I run with brainy types. I'll bet you've done things the average person could have only dreamed of."

"Thanks for trying to make me feel better."

"Any particular movie you want to see tonight?"

She hesitated. "You know what I'd really like? To go to your place and maybe watch a movie cuddled up on the couch."

"Fine by me. I have a great collection."

She followed David home and entered his recently organized apartment. "You're a great housekeeper."

"Think so?"

"You should see my place. I'm a pig compared to this." She glanced over at his computers. "I see you bring your work home."

"I have a lot of games, too."

"I'm pretty good at computer games."

"Shall we pick a movie?"

She opened her purse and removed a condom. "I have a better idea."

"I guess you do."

She caressed his shoulders and gently brushed her lips across his. David embraced her passionately and they kissed in the middle of the living room. "I want you. Let's go to the bedroom."

"It's right this way."

They tore off their clothes, fell onto the bed and indulged each other's wildest desires. After many hours, David eventually went to sleep with a satisfied grin on his face and was the first to wake up the next morning. He leaned over and gazed at his lover, who was still asleep. She awoke, rubbed her eyes and smiled. "Morning. Gee, I must look a sight."

"You look like a goddess."

"You were a tiger last night." She kissed him. "I don't have to go to work until later. What about you?"

"I don't have to go to work at all."

"Great. Then let's stay in all afternoon."

"No argument here."

David and Lesa were together almost every day and night of the week. As long as he was with her, the rebound relationship didn't matter. They agreed on a few ground rules to make each other comfortable. Lesa expressed her fear of socializing with David's intellectual crowd and he felt the same way about her Hollywood friends. They mutually agreed to put off any event that would make the other one uneasy.

David surprised her one evening with a trip to an observatory where a good friend of his was a resident astronomer. She was excited and stopped at every display case on the way to the telescope. David's friend had arranged a private viewing and allowed them to use the equipment. "This is awesome."

"Impressive, huh?"

"We're going to look at outer space?"

"Lesa, we're already in outer space."

"Oh, you mean like Earth."

He adjusted the telescope controls. "This was constructed in the 1940's."

"That's ancient history to me."

"Not that long ago." He stepped away. "Take a look."

She pressed her eye against the lens. "What is it?"

"Venus."

"That's Venus?" She peered into the lens. "It's so big."

"Big in the telescope. Earth is actually about two hundred million kilometers away right about now."

"Wow, the universe is huge."

"No question about it."

"And you say Venus is hot?"

David held her hand. "You're hot." He kissed her on the lips. "I don't know what I did to deserve you."

"You're so sweet. You always know what to say."

He sheepishly glanced away. "We're having a dinner at the college in a few days. I was wondering if you would accompany me?"

"I don't know, David. I would feel stupid around those people."

"No you wouldn't. First of all, you're better looking than all of them."

"Would you mind if I didn't go. I mean, once our relationship gets further on, then maybe it will be different."

"Okay, you don't have to go. I wish I didn't have."

At the college, Professor Maydom noticed that David had missed a lot of work and seemed to be preoccupied. He wandered over to him while he was reviewing equations. "Having trouble?"

"Just the usual anomalies and dead ends."

"David, something's been on your mind lately."

"It shows?"

"I here you've been keeping company with a young lady? And believe me, there is nothing wrong with that. I'm happy for you."

"Thank you, Charles. We've been seeing a lot of each other. But I haven't been ignoring my work."

"I didn't mean to suggest that. Sometimes a diversion can open us to new ideas that other wise we may have be missed. Love has never interfered with great science."

"That's almost poetic."

"I'm an old man. I can be poetic. I've been with Mrs. Maydon for thirty-eight years and don't regret any of it. Enjoy yourself while you're young. Mathematical calculations will always be there."

"Thanks for the encouragement."

That evening at David's apartment while he studied his formula on twin screens, Lesa was intensely involved with one of his computer games. After conquering the next level, Lesa put the controller down and hugged him from behind. "How's it going?"

He squeezed her hand. "Not so good. I'm hitting a lot of obstacles. But that's been an ongoing torture for years."

"I don't know how you stick with it."

"Science is a game of patience. Most of the time, it ends up in failure."

"It looks so complicated."

"To be honest, it really is. Problem is; nothing fits. And it has to all fit or it's not a unified equation."

"That's important, huh?"

He pointed to the screen. "These are quintic equations. I'm also using differential calculus. I have to find a combination that not only will mathematically compute, but be able to expand on itself and build on those numbers. I know this is boring to you; but at least you can understand that it all has to fit together perfectly."

"I wish I could help you."

"PI is general formula with numbers that can be computed out forever. And yet, it's not exact enough for my needs."

"All your letters and numbers look kind of pretty."

"If equations can look pretty."

"I know a neat trick. But I have to mess with your formula. Can you make a copy for me so I won't delete anything? What I do is kind of like a Photoshop."

He was amused. "Sure. It's only a partial formula anyway."

"My ex taught me some tricks."

He copied his equation. "Have at it."

She began to flip certain quadratic equations and moved around others. David was amazed that she was able to rotate individual letters and numbers; something that he didn't think possible in the computer's program.

"How did you do that?"

With the click of a button, something very unusual began to happen to her hybrid formula. The computer eliminated the equations that she reversed, but added in those letters she rotated; which should have been impossible for the program. Instead, the equation rapidly progressed and expanded even further out than his; eventually crashing the program all together.

He was stunned. "What the hell?"

"It was a copy. I couldn't have broken anything."

David's mouth opened wide. "This is phenomenal. I can't explain it. You may have just figured out the unified theory."

"Come on, you're joking. Talk to me about fashion, not math."

"You don't understand. The data does not lie." He made another copy of the original equation and then ran her program changes again. "If I'm right, this should expand and crash the computer." He entered the sequence and the numbers flew by at dizzying speeds until the error code appeared. "This is fantastic."

"I'm telling you I didn't do anything."

"This is the most incredible thing I have ever seen. When you flipped the equations, they canceled out each other; like positive and negative. But when you flipped the individual letters, it somehow quantified the other equations and solved the theory. Everything that remains aligns perfectly. Could it be that simple just eliminating some of the numbers? Whatever you did, what remains is the solution to the unified theory. I could have gone on for ten years and found nothing. You come along, tweak the program and everything fits into place. Lesa, you just solved the secrets of the universe."

"This is way over my head. But if my accident helped you, I'm thrilled."

"I'll have to run it through our super computers at the lab." He raced around the apartment to find his keys. "I got to go. Hope you don't mind? I know it's rude. But you can stay here and wait for me."

"Go. It's a big deal to you."

At six o' clock in the morning, Professor Maydon arrived at the lab and found David seated at the main computer terminal. He greeted him, but David was almost comatose. Maydon shook him, but he just stared straight ahead at the monitor. "Professor Brand, what's wrong with you?"

As if coming out of a trance, David glanced upward. "Nothing. Nothing's wrong. The equation's solved."

"What do you mean?"

"The unified theory is fact."

Maydon almost collapsed over David's chair. "What?"

"I've run it over and over. It crashes every time. There's no computer in existence that can keep up with this calculation."

"You don't mind if I verify that?"

David stood up. "Be my guest."

Maydon entered the program and confirmed that the equation had been solved. He also understood that the ramifications would be life altering. "This is beyond imagination. But how?"

"You're not going to believe it. My girlfriend solved it."

"An actress solved the equation?"

"She was demonstrating some kind of trick and then everything fell into place. It just magically fell into place."

"David, you expect me to believe a commoner solved it? That's absurd."

"She doesn't know much about history, but she made it."

"This changes everything forever. This actress has helped us achieve a quantum leap in science. But be prepared for the onslaught to come."

The television anchor interrupted regular television programming. "We have breaking news. This is Andrew Collins in New York. We have just received information that a Cal Tech scientist has just discovered the secrets of the universe. This is not a joke. David Brand has apparently discovered what is known as the unified theory and we are told that it will lead to remarkable technological advances.

We're now going to Audrey Jones of KBXT, our affiliate in Los Angeles."

"That's right, Andrew. I'm standing here in front of Cal Tech where scientist David Brand has solved one of the greatest mysteries of the universe. We are just about to have a news conference."

David Brand, Professor Maydon and a representative from NASA were seated at a table in a claustrophobic room in front of several reporters. One of them raised her hand. "Professor Brand, we understand that this could lead to many advances in space travel?"

"It will enable humans to travel beyond the stars."

Another reporter shouted out a question. "You mean faster than the speed of light?"

"I believe this discovery will lead to the knowledge where travel beyond the speed of light will be commonplace."

Professor Maydom interrupted. "I must stress that these kinds of breakthroughs take many years in the future to develop. However, now that we have the unified formula, anything is possible."

"Processor Brand, how does it feel to take your place among the greats like Newton and Einstein?"

"Humbling."

"Professor Brand, we understand that your girlfriend had something to do with this discovery?"

"All I can say now is that it was a random coincidence."

"When can we interview this woman?"

"She's asked that her name be withheld for now. Eventually she'll talk to the media. But I must stress that my equations were the lynch pin that made the discovery possible. But I couldn't have solved it without her."

"Has this equation been verified by others?"

Professor Maydon interjected. "You mean, is it another cold fusion? Several renown scientists have reviewed the data and corroborated the findings."

In the weeks to follow David had become a world wide sensation. He had been interviewed hundreds of time by various media outlets and seemed to be on every magazine cover. Success had brought him instant fame, something he found difficult at first. While his celebrity status required much of his time, he had a more pressing problem gnawing at him. He had tried phoning Lesa hundreds of times, but only received her answering machine. When that failed, he drove past her apartment, but she was never there. He visited all the clubs, but couldn't find her anywhere. He became short tempered and more miserable as each day progressed without her.

He left a message one afternoon. "Lesa, this is David. I don't know what's wrong. Why don't you answer? Did I do something? I didn't give out your name. Please answer the phone. I thought we were friends." He hung up and called once again. "Lesa, I won't be bothering you anymore. If I said something or did something, I'm sorry. I hope you have a good life." He tossed his cell phone across the room.

Distraught, he sulked inside his apartment for three days without contacting anyone. He missed a few media interviews and didn't visit the laboratory. Aware of his grief, Professor Maydon drove over to his apartment, buzzed the intercom, but was unable to gain entry. And then out of nowhere, Lesa's voice was heard over the intercom. "Hello, David. Are you there?"

He seriously contemplated ignoring her, but then opened the door. She stood before him, teary eyed and remorseful. He shook his head. "Why didn't you answer my calls? I thought we meant more to each other."

"I didn't want to hurt you."

"But you did. You hurt me bad."

"When I helped you discover the answer to the universe, it really freaked me out. I thought about the questions, the meetings; all the stuff with all those smart people. I just didn't want to feel stupid in front of them. You know that would have happened."

"Okay, so you were overwhelmed. So was I. But people who love each other make concessions. They don't just throw everything away."

She could barely make eye contact. "Oh, David. There's no easy way to say this. Sometimes these things happen. I'm going back to my ex boyfriend."

David's heart skipped a beat. "What?"

"He wants me back. I can handle his world. He promised me things will be different. I hope you understand?"

"I can't believe you'd fall for that."

"I'm sorry."

He grabbed the edge of the door. "You're nuts. Just go."

She turned away from him, left the apartment building and started walking down the street and around the corner. Her pace quickened and she gazed down at her open palm, which turned bright silver. Her entire body then lit up like the sun and she was transported to an ovular vessel with spiked protrusions from within a webbed lattice of crisscrossing lights.

She was met by another being of her kind. "I trust you were successful, Magistrate?"

"Yes, Commander."

"It's troubling we only discovered four worthy civilizations."

"We're not here to meet a quota."

"Your decision to include this planet is questionable. Considering its tendency for violence."

She smiled. "You should revisit our own history, Commander."

"You're suggesting a child's game?"

"We were much like them in our past."

"You have given them the ability to travel beyond their system."

"The human scientist deserves some credit. He was remarkably close to solving the equation. He may have eventually succeeded."

"You speak as if you were fond of him?"

"My feelings are irrelevant. I know my orders."

"Your reputation has impressed us all."

"Still, it would be interesting to monitor their future exploits."

"Your crew is anxious to complete this assignment."

"I understand. We are a long way from home. The crew has served in an exemplary manner and we're all tired." She took her place in the center of the bridge. "Prepare to reconfigure."

The pilot entered a series of commands and the vessel twisted and melded into a smaller glowing red mass with a single chain of lights rotating at high speeds. The Magistrate gave the order to depart, which caused the stars in their view screen to blur as if swept by a windshield wiper. Seconds later they reappeared in the outskirts of their solar system, where a magnificent city sparkled in the distance. They morphed back into their normal configuration and the Magistrate nodded. "We're home."

THE BOG

This was a stately coach and rig, one becoming of a doctor and his young wife traveling through Hantshire County on a bitter, damp afternoon. The driver, his coat wrapped tight against his chin, snapped the reigns to hasten the horses over the uneven road. Inside the velvet draped interior, the occupants remained in good spirits while jockeying from side to side.

"How fortunate to be the wife of Nathanial Owens."

The doctor held onto her hand. "The fortune is mine."

She smiled excitedly. "It has been a wonderful year, my love. What more could I have asked for."

The wheel dipped into a hole in the road, nearly dislodging them from their seats. "I still can't get over the fact that you consider this an ideal vacation. We could have toured the continent."

She stared out the window at the fog laden marsh. "It is exactly what I had in mind to inspire my prose."

He chuckled. "Oh yes. Your penchant for monsters and beasts of legend."

"You don't approve?"

"We wouldn't be here if I didn't approve. If this ill natured climate inspires your next tale of the macabre, far be it from to me to discourage you."

"Just look at it. So mysterious and foreboding."

"If you ask me, it's a dreary place unfit for habitation."

Another rut in the road jolted them hard enough for Doctor Owens to slide up the window and shout up to the driver. "Mr. Harbrin, how much longer?"

"Two hours, sir."

A frosty blast of air entered the cab. "Are you certain?"

"Yes sir. But there's a town up ahead. Dorsten."

He shouted back up to him. "Inquire about lodging for the night." Shivering, he closed the window.

"Fabulous idea, Nathanial. We've been on this road for a while. Staying in New Forest should overwhelm me with fresh ideas."

The driver pulled back on the reigns when Dorsten appeared around the bend. They turned off the road and the horses traversed the cobblestone streets through a village of thatch roofs, a center square with garden and a church with a prominent steeple. The townsfolk blissfully sauntered along the pavement and graciously nodded at them.

The driver halted the coach in the square, dismounted, opened the door and immediately exposed Doctor Owens and his wife to the inhospitable weather. A man with a frayed brown hat and unkempt facial whiskers approached them. "Welcome, my friends. The name's Louden Fink. I'm mayor of Dorsten."

"Doctor Owens. This is my wife, Lucy."

He extended his hand. "Nice to meet you, Doc. And Mrs. Owens."

"It's getting late and we were hoping to find lodging."

"We can help you with that. Abigail Peckenpipple manages the Inn. There's comfortable rooms and warm fireplaces."

"That should suffice."

The driver pointed at the wheel. "I noticed some friction. Do you have someone that can repair this?"

"Just the best smith in these parts. He'll fix you up in no time. Let's gather your bags. The Inn's just over there."

"Mr. Harbrin, I'll arrange a room for you. We'll see to the luggage."

"Thank you, sir."

Mayor Fink picked up two bags. "Just one thing, Doc. I'd advise you not to have supper at the Inn. Abigail Peckenpipple's cooking isn't exactly what I'd call edible. She does bake acceptable biscuits and jam for breakfast."

"Then what do you suggest? We're hungry."

"The Baby Rose tavern. Rose Tolliver, proprietor. She's the best cook in town. That is, next to my Emily. I'll come by later and take you there myself."

Lucy followed him. "Thank you."

"I might pay my respects to your doctor."

"We don't have a doctor."

"I understand; this being a small town."

"We manage, all right."

"You must rely on a traveling physician. If he should visit, don't hesitate to notify me. I should like to pay my respects."

Mayor Fink stopped in front of a two story cottage. "Here we are. Welcome to the Peckenpipple Inn."

Though British, the owner of the Inn was a stout woman with Germanic features. She was exceedingly cordial and spoke with a kind voice. The mayor dropped the luggage on the creaky wooden floor and then warmed his hands by the fireplace.

"I'm Doctor Owens. This is my wife Lucy."

"Welcome to my home."

The mayor pitched chunks of wood into the fireplace, blasting embers up the funnel shaft. "They'll be needing two rooms."

Abigail turned the signing book towards Doctor Owens. "I have two that should suffice. Will you be joining us for dinner?"

The mayor quickly interrupted. "Oh, ahh, no they won't. They'll be dining with me this evening."

"Very well. This way." Abigail picked up a lantern and brushed right past them up the stairs.

The driver entered the front door just in time and followed them. As promised the beds were soft and the fireplace was stacked with a bundle of dry wood. Abigail lit the oil lamps and drew back the curtains. "If you need anything, don't hesitate to ask."

"Thank you." Lucy closed the door and Nathanial peered out the window. "The county's scattered with these little hamlets."

"They're lovely."

"Somewhat austere, if you ask me." He wandered over to the fireplace. "I'll get this started. It's a bit chilly."

"The bog is a perfect setting for my new novel."

"If you say so, my dear. Personally, I can't wait to get home."

"Come now, Nathanial. Isn't it good to get away from your patients for a while?"

"Point well taken."

As promised Mayor Fink arrived at the Inn and escorted them across town to the tavern which had an emblem of a green wreath surrounding a red rose painted overhead. Though it was nothing more than an average pub, the owner was well known for her culinary arts. Inside the folks were listening to local musicians, tossing darts and drinking the finest ale in town.

The mayor rapped his knuckles on one of the tables and demanded everyone's attention. "Excuse me, but we have honored guests tonight. This is the Doc Owens, and his wife Lucy."

They were slightly embarrassed when a few patrons rushed over and greeted them with extended hands. Rose Tolliver, a fair haired young woman, brought over two steins of ale. Lucy waved her hand. "I'll have tea. My husband will enjoy the ale."

Rose wiped her hands on a towel around her waist. "Then tea it is. You both be hungry, I hope."

"That they are, Rose. What are you serving?"

"My specialty. Stew."

Lucy smiled. "We're famished."

The mayor brought them over to his favorite table. "Sit down, Doc. Wait until you taste the fare. Doesn't get any better."

Rose returned with a basket of hot bread and two steamy bowls. Doctor Owens sniffed the broth and the aroma delighted his senses. "If this tastes as good as it smells, I should be quite satisfied."

"Rose has never had a complaint."

Lucy followed with a sip of her own. "It's marvelous. Simply marvelous."

The mayor toasted his guests. "Here's to a lovely couple." The tavern's occupants joined in with raised glasses. "So, I've been meaning to ask you folks. What brings you to Hantshire county?"

"It was my wife's idea. She wanted inspiration for her novel."

Lucy chewed on a tender piece of meat. "I'm particularly interested in the bogs."

The mayor, along with the rest of the patrons, suddenly froze and stared at them with penetrating eyes. "Is there a problem?" inquired Doctor Owens, perplexed at what he considered a bizarre reaction.

"You mustn't go into the bog."

"Why?"

"It's dangerous. There is unspeakably evil."

Doctor Owens was surprised and amused. "You can't be serious?"

"The bog is a home for demons."

"My good man, that kind of talk is superstitious at best. There are perhaps wolves and adders, but I seriously doubt anything beyond that. My hunting rifle should make quick work of them."

"You don't understand, Doc. There are creatures in that bog that no human weapon can destroy."

"Nonsense."

"The bog is evil, I tell ya. No place for you and your Misses."

Lucy tried to calm everyone's fears. "I appreciate all your concerns. However, New Forest is a perfect setting for my novel. The mood is simply enchanting. My husband will take precautions."

A gruffly old man with a patchwork coat smacked the top of the table. "Never mind, Mayor. I'll take them into the bog. They seem to be quite determined."

"That's Edmund Parish. Don't listen to him, Doc."

Edmund stood up. "You're all a bunch of cowards."

The mayor aimed his thumb at him. "Mr. Parish digs for peat. He works the edges of the bog."

"Aye, that's right. And I don't underestimate it. It's haunted, all right. There are many dangers. But I have talismans and charms to keep us safe."

Doctor Owens was incredulous. "I'll give you two quid to show us around."

"Three and I'll do it."

"You have a deal."

"I'll come by tomorrow morning."

The mayor covered Lucy's hand with his. "You shouldn't go in there. You don't have any special powers over demons."

"I shall be careful."

By morning a wet mist settled over the streets as Nathanial and Lucy enjoyed Abigail's tasty biscuits. Half way through the meal, Edmund Parish barreled through the front door carrying an assortment of beads and charms. Doctor Owens chuckled while spreading jam on his biscuit. "I see you've come prepared, my good man. However, I will have my hunting rifle by my side."

"Suit yourself, Doc." He turned to Lucy. "Perhaps you would be interested?"

She selected one of the necklaces. "Thank you, Mr. Parish. I shall feel much safer with this."

"You don't have to go with us, Mrs. Owens."

"Actually, I do. My novel has its share of monsters."

Mr. Harbrin brought the coach up to the Inn. After Edmund gave directions to the driver, they headed down the road. When they reached the preferred location of entry, Parish banged his fist on the ceiling and draped several charms around his neck. "From now on, these will be our only salvation."

Doctor Owens instructed the driver to wait for them. "No use delaying the inevitable, Mr. Parish." Edmund led the way into a blanket of fog that swirled around their ankles. He called out ahead to warn them of the muddier pools winding through the higher mounds of flattened grass. "Mr. Parish, I detect a mild odor of sulfur."

"That's from hell, Doc."

"Nathanial, I shall enjoy describing that foul odor."

"That pleases me, my dear." He muttered to himself. "Bloody rot."

Edmund held up his hand and then with palpable fear pointed down at the water. "The bubbling mud!"

"Oh, for heaven's sakes. It's marsh gasses."

He tugged on Doctor Owens' coat sleeve. "No, it's the bubbling mud. Those that come near are dragged down to hell itself."

"Is that really possible?"

"Stay clear."

Doctor Owens searched for a fallen twig and stuck it into the rising bubbles. Parish leaped back and held his hand over his mouth. Owens swished the twig around the water and glanced over at him. "See, nothing happens. It's just natural gasses."

"Perhaps my talisman is protecting you from afar."

"There is nothing demonic about this mud."

Lucy laid her hand on his shoulder. "I appreciate you protecting my husband, Mr. Parish. I'm inclined to believe it was your talisman that did the trick."

"Don't mention it. He's lucky I'm here."

Owens tossed the twig away. "Ridiculous."

They trudged further into the bog, drenching their boots up to their shins. They meticulously pushed aside thorny shrubbery to avoid the deeper pools. The fog seemed to thicken and Parish became frightened and agitated. He suddenly halted their progress. "Look, out there! Beyond that rock."

Owens raised his rifle. "What do you see?"

"It's the smoke beast!"

"It's fog."

"No, it's the beast, and it's beginning to form. Soon its blood red eyes will pierce through your heart."

Lucy once again tried to calm him down. "I'm fairly sure it's fog, Mr. Parish. I don't believe it's a threat to us."

"Never underestimate the smoke beast."

"Ohhh . . . bloody hell." Owens charged the fog and vanished into its thickest layers. He trampled along the base of a low lying knoll and returned to them unharmed. "Just as I suspected. Ordinary fog, nothing more."

"I've seen the smoke beast. You are lucky to be alive."

"Luck as nothing to do with it. Please lead on."

A wolf's howl echoed in the distance. Lucy, who had been unconcerned up until now, was troubled by their calls. "Nathanial?"

"Well, Mr. Parish? What manner of beast must we now contend with?"

"It's a wolf. We're in no danger from a wolf. It's a flesh and blood creature. Besides, you have a gun."

Exasperated, Doctor Owens' shoulders lunged upward. "You're afraid of the fog, but not a wolf. Why can't you understand that there is nothing haunted in the bog? Just the basic elements of nature." He turned to his wife. "Lucy, have you seen enough?"

"I believe so."

"Good. Then . . ."

Edmund fell to his knees, cried out in utter terror and pointed at a slightly elevated bank of tall reeds. "We're doomed!"

Doctor Owens concentrated on an area where some kind of animal had poked its head out of the vegetation. "It's a donkey, my good man."

"No, it's the two headed donkey. A fierce beast that takes no prisoners."

"Is this some kind of jest on your part?"

Lucy helped Mr. Parish up to his feet. "It's a donkey, Mr. Parish."

Nathanial snickered. "Anyway, this only has one head."

"You don't understand. It grows another head and attacks you."

"Nice. A two headed bog monster."

"We should leave, now."

"Right. That's it." Doctor Owens charged the animal, which immediately retreated in haste. He rambled towards them, brushing splotches of mud off his pants. "I told you it was just a wild donkey."

"Doc, it looks like my charms held off another beast."

"Do you seriously believe your charms abated a stupid donkey?"

After the excursion, Mr. Harbrin, who had been waiting for them along the roadside, brought them back to the center square. Mayor Fink and some of the townsfolk seemed truly astonished that they were still alive. "Doc, you made it back." The others surrounded them and muttered quietly to each other.

"Of course we returned. As I told you previously, there is nothing supernatural in the bog. It's just a wet miserable place."

"Did you see the bubbling mud?"

"Saw the bubbling mud."

"I don't know how you survived. But it pleases me."

Edmund spoke proudly. "It was my talisman. Saved us from the two headed donkey."

"You saw the donkey?"

"Saw the donkey."

"Not many live after seeing the donkey."

Lucy smiled at their tenuous faces. "We have lived through the experience of the bog. And I have what I need."

"That's fine, Mrs. Owens. But it's getting late. The demons will be out tonight."

"Mayor Fink, my husband is correct. The bog is harmless."

A young man with blond locks pushed his way through the crowd. "They wouldn't be so brave if they saw the death tree."

Everybody hushed up and held on to each other. The mayor's eyes widened. "Don't even mention the death tree."

"All right, I have to ask. What is the death tree?"

"You don't want anything to do with that, Doc. It sits alone on top of a hill. It's the most powerful demon of them all."

"So the bog has a death tree."

The young man dismissed his arrogance. "You sound brave now, Doctor Owens. But once you confront the death tree, you'll change your mind."

"Let's go see that tree of yours."

The young man strutted up to the coach. "I'll show you it myself."

The mayor was genuinely puzzled by Nathanial's bravado. "Doc, it's getting late. The bog is too dangerous now."

Rose Tolliver approached Lucy. "Before you go anywhere, allow me to prepare a meal for the both of you."

Doctor Owens scoffed at her. "Are you suggesting a last meal?"

"No, a warm meal. I just want a word with you before you venture into the bog again."

In the tavern Rose brought them each a plate of sizzling pork and a boiled potato. After a few bites, Rose sat down next to them and spoke solemnly. "There's something you should know about the bog and the death tree."

"Here it comes."

"I see you're skeptical."

"You'll have to forgive me. I'm a man of science."

"I must admit that I never experienced anything unusual in the bog. I inherited this tavern from my father. He raised me after my mother died. He told me stories that the death tree had taken several of his friends."

"And you believed him?"

"Well, they never came back. They say the tree is guarding some kind of treasure. I'm not telling you this to frighten you. I just want you to weigh the possibility that these stories are true."

Lucy swallowed a forkful of potato. "I don't have to see the tree, Nathanial. I've seen enough."

"But I haven't. I want to prove to all of Dorsten that this tree is just another superstitious myth. I shall take that young man up on his offer."

Rose stood up. "It's your decision."

"Lucy, I understand if you wish to remain behind."

"Oh no, I'm going."

Soon after sunset the young man rode his horse ahead of the coach and tied it to a wooden fence next to the edges of the bog. The moon, now half glowing from behind a veil of thin clouds, teased them with minimal traces of light. Doctor Owens grabbed his rifle and helped Lucy off the step.

"You really want to bring your wife along?"

"She's old enough to make her own decisions."

"Not to worry. My husband will protect me."

Doctor Owens picked up a lantern. "Mr. Harbrin. Wait for us here. We shall return shortly."

The young man waved his lantern above his head. "The death tree has many arms. It drags its victims down to the fires of hell."

"Then off to hell it is."

"You're proud. Much too proud. Pride cometh before the fall."

"So be it."

The young man chose a path over the higher grassy mounds where their heels plunged into the muddier pools.

Lucy followed her husband closely, but stood motionless when several wolves howled in unison."

"Damn animals. Don't have to worry about them."

He held up his weapon. "I'm not worried in the least." The rustling in the thickets ahead indicated there may be a roaming pack. Doctor Owens aimed the gun high and delivered one shot, which frightened them. "They won't be bothering us any longer."

"I'm grateful you didn't have to harm them, dear."

Doctor Owens sniffed the air. "There's that Sulfur again."

"The smell of death tree."

"No, that's what causes the mud to boil."

The young man pushed away dense brush and they emerged into an area of sparse foliage where a lone dead tree towered ominously on a nearby hill. The myriad of branches stretched out like sharp crooked arms suggesting an aura of wickedness.

"So that's the infamous death tree."

"I wouldn't go any farther, Doc."

"Is that so?" He turned to his wife. "Lucy, I see no reason for you to make the hike. Stay here with the lad."

Lucy smiled at her husband. "Be careful. Don't slip."

"It's your last chance, Owens. Don't be a fool."

"Is it foolish to prove to the good people of Dorsten that this is just an ordinary birch tree? And dead at that. I'm doing your hamlet a little favor."

He passed the gun to his wife and plodded up the side of the short hill. Though loose rocks tumbled from beneath his boots, he was able to keep his balance by clutching onto secured twigs and stringy vegetation. His lantern provided some light, but the silhouette of the tree was often obscured when the clouds hid the moonlight.

He arrived at the top of a flattened mound, turned his back away from the tree and shouted down to them. "Here I am. Safe for the moment."

The young man reared back. "He's a goner."

Lucy held his hand. "Don't fret. My husband will be fine."

"I'm not so sure."

Owens faced the trunk. "All right, tree of death. I'm here. Take me. Ahh, but you can't. Because you're just a tree." Amused by the absurdity, he slapped his forehead. "Here I am, talking to a tree."

The young man hollered up to him. "Save yourself, Doc!"

Nathanial ripped off a piece of bark. He held it high over his head. "I'm still here. I'm still alive"

"He's damaged the tree!"

Lucy comforted him. "If this were really a death tree, would it allow my husband do that?"

"He's marked for death."

Doctor Owens tossed the bark on the ground, rubbed his hands and was about to climb back down the hill when a low lying branch tore into his coat along the shoulder. The young man screamed in horror and ran away. Lucy called out to her husband who was immobilized. Nathanial simply clutched onto the branch, snapped it in two and hiked down the hillside. "Ruined a perfectly good coat."

"Sorry, my love. They must have a tailor in town."

"What happened to the lad?"

"The excitement was too much for him."

"I trust you've had enough?"

"Yes. I believe we've disturbed enough demons for the night."

They trekked back through the marsh and found Mr. Harbrin exactly where they had left him. When the young man had failed to retrieve his horse, Doctor Owens ordered Harbrin to return to town. For some reason the coach stopped before reaching the Inn and Nathanial banged on the ceiling. "What now?" When there was no response, he opened the window and called out to Harbrin. "Is there a problem?" There was still no response, so he opened the door.

It was eerily quiet and the townsfolk seem to be missing. And then out of nowhere a parade of short, hairy creatures with clawed hands, dagger like ears, long pointy noses and protruding fangs began roaming the streets. Lucy stepped outside and immediately held onto her husband's arm. As if everything was routine, the creatures strolled along the pavement, greeted one another and browsed through the shops.

"What is happening, Nathanial?"

"I don't have a clue."

One of the creatures traipsed right up to them. Doctor Owens stepped in front of his wife to protect her. "What is it you want?"

The creature stared oddly. "It's me, Doc. The mayor."

"The mayor?"

"Is everything all right?"

"What manner of being are you?"

"It's difficult to keep up the illusion. But I assure you, I'm Louden Fink"

"So you're actually . . ."

"Goblins."

"And you come from the bog?"

"Absolutely not. We live here in town."

Doctor Owens carefully selected his next words. "I suppose we're going to die?"

"Not unless you plan on eating at the Inn tonight?"

"Then you're not going to kill us?"

"Kill you? Why would we do that, Doc.? We like you. Besides, you haven't broken any laws, have you?"

"But you're goblins."

"Law abiding goblins, I may add. Look Doc, it's getting late. If we make you uncomfortable, you can leave anytime. But I'd advise against it. It's dangerous in the bog at night."

"Mayor Fink, there is no danger in the bog."

You're lucky to have survived the death tree."

"Oh please, not the death tree again."

"Stay with us here tonight. My wife and I would be honored if you joined us. We're having a few friends over. Your driver's welcome, too. You can leave in the morning when it's safer." He gazed down the street and shuttered. "The night is no place for the bog."

"Mayor, I'm telling you there's nothing in the . . ."

Lucy gently tugged on her husband's arm, pursed her lips, shook her head and whispered, "no, no, no." She smiled warmly at the mayor. "We would be delighted to be your guests this evening."

"Good show."

Doctor Owens glanced up at his driver. "Mr. Harbrin, let's not be rude. We're accepting our host's invitation."

They followed the mayor towards his house and Lucy nestled her head against her husband's shoulder. "This has been an interesting vacation. I have all I need to write a scary tale. That is, without mentioning anything about this town."

"Yes, I suppose even the best of goblins deserve their privacy."

EXCHANGE

My name is Carl Becktow. My great grandparents were the last generation of my family to be born on Earth before the war made the planet uninhabitable. Most say that if wormhole technology had not been discovered, the human race would have become extinct. But that didn't happen. We had successfully established off world colonies in other systems. I was born on the planet Drexo 5, so named after some long dead historical figure. There are five other planets in the system, two of them belonging to another species known as the Ibrata. Presently I'm sitting in a holding room of sorts on a space station midway between planets. I am waiting to be exiled to Ibrata for crimes against my people. I'm told there is an Ibratan awaiting the same fate. But enough about my future. It's time to look into the past and how I got here. Fortunately for me, many books and historical accounts survived from the Earth and are readily available for viewing. Such was a book called 1984 by George Orwell. His real name was Eric Blair and he was some kind of reporter. I don't know why Orwell picked that year, but

I'm certain the year is irrelevant. What's amazing is that our government even allowed this book to exist. Orwell writes that "he who controls the past, controls the future". Now you ask, why would my government allow that proclamation to persist in these times? It's because they are immune to such hypocrisy. They simply point to a chaotic past full of worldly annihilation to justify their concept of the future. And that is where my story begins. Now let me make myself clear. This is not a political rant, a philosophical or religious dissertation. And systems like facism, communism, capitalism and monarchies were old style labels. Anyway, I don't know what the differences really were. But I will tell you I live in a world where the government is everything. It absolutely controls everything and is the final arbitrator. It's the law, the economy, the religion and its power is unchallenged. I was born a citizen of Drexo 5 and have a mother, father and one younger brother. My mother and father were appointed to work by the Department of Work Selection. Something about that Department. They administer several tests throughout one's youth and no one is ever provided with the results or allowed to protest. My mother and father, like most citizens, were given jobs in the factories. They worked on an assembly line making artificial waterfalls. They would do that for the rest of their lives. After their shift, they went home to their government assigned home. Every citizen is told where to live. And when one attains a certain age, they are sent into retirement where your family is not allowed to visit. It's not considered cruel, because everybody receives the same kind of treatment. That's the way it is. Everybody rejoices and everybody suffers the same. I loved my parents and I missed them when they went away. But they never complained. That's the thing about Drexo 5. No one ever complains. You're taught at an early age to obey the government and never question its laws. And there are many laws. Now I did well in school. I was beaten only once for missing a school lunch period. After three beatings, you are subjected to a period of shunning. Believe me, shunning is far worse than the beating. Not even your parents can speak to you. That wouldn't be the last time I suffered such a fate. But I avoided most of that kind of thing. I excelled in school and must have impressed the Department of Selection on all those tests. When I graduated, I was placed in the Department of Science. That is one of the most prestigious positions one can obtain. Of course being a member of the government class is the most honorable position. To reach that level, one must have connections. But I don't want to get into that aspect of society at this time. So I belong to the Department of Science which has been responsible for all the technological advancements: space travel, medicine, new inventions. So there I was an unhappy twenty year old scientist because that year my mother and father were remanded to the retirement home. Our laws of retirement are heartless. The house I was raised in was no longer mine. The government givith, the government taketh away. Nobody ever complains, nobody ever resists. By the way, it's a crime to be unhappy. You can be sent to prison for it. Can you imagine that, the government even insists on happiness. They insist on controlling emotions. So who is the government? That brings me back to Orwell. Truth be told, if one is not allowed to question their government, then no one will ever know who the government is. And that is why I am ignorant of my enemy. Oh there's a council of seven that have ultimate authority. Under them is a committee for another committee for another committee.

The courts mediate them, but the courts are part of the government. You'll find them in the Department of Committees. So I was a promising scientist and with that came excellent benefits. The government assigned me to a beautiful house in an upper class neighborhood. I had a job and a house and it was time to find a mate. The government selects a mate for each person. They know what companion is best for you and you'd better be happy. A farmer marries a farmer, a factory worker marries a factory worker and a scientist marries a scientist. So I was introduced to my wife, Louisa. She was attractive, but I was not attracted to her at first. Louisa was cold, distant, and without humor. But we managed to find common ground and we actually became fond of one another. We had two children, a boy and a girl. Louisa was a superb scientist and mother and really cared for her family. But the children were taught the rules early on, and like everybody else, they obeyed according to the law. And don't deceive yourself, your children will turn you in. I remember when I first began to question the government. Louisa would hear nothing of it, so I kept it mostly to myself. She was a strong believer in the system, as were most citizens. But I wasn't. The government was cruel and it valued austerity over mercy. Pointing this out was a serious crime. So I finally began to consider revolution. Let me tell you something about revolution. Most revolutions are selfish and misguided. Perhaps my revolution is also flawed. But I don't care because I'm not the living, but the dead. My revolution is against injustice and I must not fail. So here I'm going to spend some time on crime and punishment. There is a department for that. The least crime is to disobey the rules of domestic and interplanetary travel. If one even alters their route, then the public is allowed to enter a raffle to whip you. Most citizens seem to take delight in that. The more serious crimes are disobedience to authority. We have a police force called the Badge. They are everywhere and they monitor every camera. The Badge has ultimate power and can never be questioned. We have no freedom. We are essentially slaves. Since there is no death penalty of which the government deems barbaric, the more serious crimes of murder, rape and theft are dealt with by jail terms and shaming. As I mentioned before, when one has been declared shamed, no one may even look at them. Even your family is taken from you. But there is one crime that is so heinous, so destructive to society, it is considered the most serious of all. And that is treason. It is inconceivable to the government that one could betray them. There is only one sentence for such a crime. Exile without the hope of rehabilitation. And there is a specific destination where you are sent. And so my life of treason begins at work where a few of us dared to speak about the ills of society. We kept it quiet. We knew the repercussions. I soon became familiar with a fellow scientist named Felix Gant. We had always known that the government infiltrates every part of society, and that includes the work place. But Felix was very careful and in our line of work, it was much easier to spot the infiltrators. There were a few of them over the years and were easily detected because they did not possess certain scientific knowledge. Felix began to speak of his friends that belonged to a group of freedom seeking individuals. They were called the Tribune Partnership of America. I went to my first meeting and I was home. Everyone thought like me and we would talk about this former country called America and how they once had freedom. When I was a child, I remembered my grandfather talking about America. Of course he was later retired and I never saw him again. My revolution had to start somewhere. But first you have to know who the enemy is. It's not industry, the farmers, the factory workers. Even if the people don't realize it, the enemy is the government. My wife began to ask me where I was going all the time. Fortunately men are encouraged to join in the patriotic game of Dobemin One. My wife was grateful and satisfied that I took such an interest in patriotism. We would meet after the games. Felix Gant came up with all sorts of ways to meet without getting attention from the Badge. I can't tell you how much joy I got from my discussions of freedom with Gant. He was a visionary. He spoke of the day when our children might have the ability to choose their own destinies. We wanted revolution and we even drew up our manifesto. The Tribune Partnership of America was growing and flourishing under Gant's leadership. For the first time in my life I felt empowered. Our message was beginning to take hold. We emphasized the end of group think, blind obedience to the state, the abolishment of laws, the abolishment of all the government Departments, the abolishment of the Badge, and most importantly, the right to chose one's mate. How wonderful that would be if my children could fall in love with the one that they chose. But there was talk among the neighbors about this subversive group that eventually became a concern for the government. That's when it all came to an end. The dream was over. I arrived home from work one day and my family was gone. The Badge was there to arrest me and they threw me in a dark cell. After a rather lengthy beating, I must have stayed in the cell for many weeks. The next time I even saw light was at my trial. They walked me to a court and stood me in front of the entire state to see.

My wife and children were there, but as protocol dictated, they were compelled to look away from me and stare at the wall. For them it was fortunate that it was my crime, not their's. It was a short trial and after that I never saw them again. My chief accuser turned out to be my friend and mentor, Felix Gant. He was the infiltrator. They were that good. I was a small fish in a big pond and didn't realize it. There I was, accused of treason, the most serious crime of all. The Tribune Partnership of America was a false organization. That hurt the most because it was such a glorious idea. Felix Gant was a member of the Department of Infiltration and he was a true patriot in the eyes of the government. My sentence was exile. And this brings me to the final chapter of my life's story. Funny thing about exile, one is taken out of society, never to be rehabilitated or forgiven. Many years ago our government made contact with another planet called Ibrata. And as I mentioned earlier, I am seated in a room awaiting exile to that planet. They are said to be a human species much like us, with some minor anatomical differences. And while they certainly didn't originate from Earth, we were compelled by our governments to learn each other's languages at a very young age. But we have never been allowed to commingle with them. So the only thing we know about each other has been from whispers or rumors. I'm told our societies are completely different and that our worlds are repulsive to one another. I go to a world of isolationists and stoics. I will be alone and will be subjected to their laws. But in my mind, I wonder what can be worse than Drexo 5. I've lost my family and I've lost my identity. So here I sit in this caged room with two guards and nobody else, awaiting the journey to Ibrata. I haven't had contact with anyone. I'm in a space station somewhere in the middle between two worlds. But I do hope that my people will one day have their revolution. I just won't be there to see it. Amidst all the pain, torture, loss of citizenship and most distressingly loss of my family, what else can happen to me? If anyone reads this document, my name is Carl Becktow and I am completely alone.

He sat on the cold steel bench and wondered what was going on in the minds of his two guards. Hours of silence passed and it seemed he would never depart from this netherworld. And then the silence was broken by noises on the other side of the door. Two more guards escorted what he perceived must have been an Ibratan citizen. The guards spoke briefly to the other guards and then the Ibratan sat down next to Becktow. He recognized Carl as a citizen of Drexo 5 and spoke to him in English. "You're not the first person I've ever met from your planet."

"But you're definitely the first Ibratan I've ever met."

"So human, what did you do to deserve this?"

"They say I am a criminal to be exiled to your planet."

"My former planet. My destination is Drexo 5."

Carl's head dropped in sorrow. "Then you are to be most pitied."

"Pitied? Why?"

"You and I are political prisoners. Our lives are considered expendable. We are without hope. Is that not the very definition of pity?"

The Ibratan was unusaully enthusiastic. "But I am looking forward to this exile. I only could have dreamed of going to Drexo 5."

"You must be delusional. Drexo 5 is a nightmare."

"On the contrary, one of your citizens told me all about it. He was exiled five years ago. He said his society was structured, authoritarian, with laws and consequences for every action."

Becktow was flabbergasted. "That's a perfect description. Drexo 5 is evil. The government lords over everything. It tells you how to behave and punishes you if you don't follow the rules."

He closed his eyes in delirium. "Then it's true. That is exactly what I was hoping for.

"You want that?"

"You don't know what it's like on my planet. We have no government to speak of. There's no direction. There's so much peace and tranquility, I'm going out of my mind. There is no incentive to be productive, no self worth, no goals to aspire to. No resistance to anything. The same thing, day after day."

"You must be joking?"

"This is no joke. My planet is dysfunctional, lazy and careless."

"You don't know what you're saying. My world is brutal, unforgiving. One mistake, one violation of the rules and you pay for it dearly."

"But at least you know the rules. You have established boundaries."

"You're a fool, Ibratan. Your exile will be unpleasant. There is no individuality. There is no creativity."

He leaned back with an exalted grin. "Everything I've ever dreamed of. If I were to stay on my planet one more day, I would have gone out of my mind." He began to laugh. "You'll find out. I'm the lucky one. I'm going to a good place."

There was another commotion by the door and three other guards rushed into the room, grabbed the Ibratan by the shoulders and took him away. The two remaining guards were mystified. "What's happening?"

"He wasn't supposed to be in here with Becktow. Somebody's going a pay a high price for making that mistake."

"They only had contact for a moment."

"I suppose no harm was done. Where they're going, it won't matter." He pointed at Becktow. "Get him ready. His transport departs shortly."

The guard walked over to him. You heard him. Let's go."

Carl was escorted down a long corridor and into a docking area exposed to the vacuum of space. He entered a shuttle craft which left the station at a high speed towards Ibrata. An hour later the shuttle landed on the surface next to a mildly rippled blue lake. In the distance was a flock of birds which dipped into a beautiful valley beyond the trees. Carl stepped out of the shuttle and watched it lift out of sight. He was alone, facing a bright star that gloriously warmed his skin.

After a while a male Ibratan approached him from around a low lying hillside. "Are you Carl Becktow?"

"I am."

"My name is Aru. I am your guide."

"You mean guard?"

"No. Guide."

"You're not taking me to prison?"

"We have no prisons here. You are an enemy of your state, not ours. I'm sorry for your loss and exile, but you will have freedom here."

"I don't understand."

"Come walk with me to your new home."

They embarked on a solitary path to a quaint village on the other side of the hill. When he saw the townspeople going about their lives with leisurely contentment, it was more than he could have hoped for. On the outskirts of the village, everyone smiled at him as they frolicked uninterrupted in their desired pursuits.

"We hope that you will be happy here."

"This is all hard to believe. And I won't be locked up?"

"No one is incarcerated. We have no crime amongst each other. Crime is an act of jealousy, covetousness. On Ibrata, one has everything they need. It's true that each town deals with internal problems as they arise. Since banishment is not pleasant, why would anyone put themselves in that position?"

"Then I am the luckiest man alive."

"Look around you, Mr. Becktow. Do you see anyone here that is distressed?"

He noticed a pretty young girl smiling at him. "Quite the opposite."

"I understand that we are foreign to your way of thinking. And you must have so many questions. But I feel once you become part of this community; the answers to those questions will satisfy your curiosity."

"You must have a military? How can you protect yourselves from outsiders?"

"We have volunteers that take on the tasks of defending our planet. Long ago we developed defensive weapons to thwart our enemies. But even those citizens enjoy the benefits of our society." He pointed over at two pretty young women. "I believe they want to have sexual relations with you."

"Is that allowed?"

"Everything is allowed. We live for pleasure. I have only one warning for you, Mr. Becktow. Don't try to form any groups that do things. We don't like the organizing types. I know that Drexo 5 is like that."

He waved his hands negatively. "You don't have to worry about that. I'm the last person on Ibrata that wants to organize anything. I like it just the way it is." He caught the eye of a maiden and ran off to catch her.

BUTTON

Vaughn Cordegat was an inquisitive nine year old child. He was a genius and sometimes his family didn't appreciate that. His bedroom was like most boys his age, except for a clutter of scientific gadgets and inventions. He was always making some kind of device, but it all seemed to be a mess for his mother, who like all moms begged him to clean his room. One day Vaughn had accidentally created a device that would set off a chain reaction that would destroy the entire galaxy. He set it aside and went off to visit his family doctor for a check-up.

The house was empty when Vaughn's older brother Gordy and his two friends got home from school and raided the refrigerator. They consumed a gallon of milk, dozens of cookies, frozen pizza; just about anything they could get their hands on. Later on they headed up to Gordy's room, but were intrigued by the sight of his brother's messy domain. "Dude, let's go in here."

Gordy shook his head. "There's nothing in there but junk."

His other friend went inside. "Looks like some rad stuff in here."

Gordy nodded. "Okay."

"Dude, I've never seen so many dork toys."

"My brother's a moron."

One friend picked up a multi-layered device. "What's this stupid thing?" He dropped it. "Slam!"

The other friend picked up a square base with plastic tubes. "Dude, it's a bong."

Gordy chuckled. "Yeah, my brother with a bong."

"Your brother's not normal."

"Tell me about it."

One of them discarded several shirts and underwear on the floor and found a plain metal box with a red button on top of it. "What's this?"

Gordy took it away from him and examined it. "Dude, I don't know. Just a box."

"What's it do?"

"How should I know." He handed it back to his friend. "Why don't you push it and find out."

He held it up and pushed the button. "Hey, nothing's hap

TRAJECTORY

Beth Anderson woke up to her husband's alarm clock and nudged him when he didn't respond. He slowly reached for the button, slammed his hand down on it, rolled over and cuddled up next to her. She smiled, and then yawned. "Good morning, baby."

He gently caressed her arm. "This is a big day for you."

"Just routine. Three senators and the President's representative."

"And they're all there to meet the African American woman that's going to save the world."

She stretched out her arms and sat on the edge of the bed. "It's not like I'm the only one on this project."

"No, but you're the brainchild."

"I hate that expression." She yawned and stretched again. "Senators or not, the kids have to go to school."

"You get Leah. I'll get Tawnee."

Damian Anderson lumbered towards his nine year old daughter's bedroom where she was still asleep under a wall of teenage posters. He leaned over her and gently shook her arm. "Wake up, honey."

Tawnee moaned at him. "Not now . . ."

He pulled off her covers. "No arguments."

Beth entered six year old Leah's room. She was already awake. "Hi mommy."

"Good morning, sweetie. You're such a joy in the morning. I wish your sister was like that."

"Can I have pancakes?"

"Frozen ones."

"Can't daddy make some?"

"Only on the weekends. How about cereal?"

"Okay." She leaped out of bed.

While Damian was showering, Beth filled two bowls with cereal. Tawnee shoved a piece of paper towards her. "You got to sign this, mom."

"Oh, that parent teacher conference."

"I wish you didn't have to go."

Beth frowned at her. "Why would you say that? You're an excellent student."

Damian, now dressed in a suit and tie, rushed into the kitchen holding his briefcase. "No time to eat. Tawnee, you ready?"

"Yeah, daddy." She gulped down her last spoonful of cereal.

He kissed Beth. "Good luck, today." He kissed his youngest daughter on the forehead and headed out the door.

Beth gazed over at Leah. "It's just you and me, baby."

Beth dropped her daughter off at school and then drove fifteen miles to the Johnson Space Center. She showed her identification badge at the main gate and parked in a personalized space. Unchallenged when displaying her credentials, she gained access to a high security site and was greeted by her young male assistant tapping on an Ipad. "What so you have for me, Stuart?"

"Senator Blakey's already here. Senator's Chase and Greenfeld should arrive any moment. Defense Secretary Halverson should arrive soon after."

"I need some coffee."

"Coffee and sweet roles in your office."

"Stuart, you're a life saver."

An hour later, Beth escorted her important guests through the hallways of the space center. Senator Chase, an old southern gentleman who had met Beth before, gazed at her like a proud father. "You see this young scientist, here. She's practically running NASA."

"I wouldn't go that far, Senator."

"Don't be modest, young lady. You've accomplished great things."

Beth stopped at a door and swiped her card. "I might be the chief designer of this project, but my staff has been instrumental in its development. Without them, this would not have been possible."

They breezed through another hallway and Senator Greenfeld cleared his throat. "I understand you have a husband and two children?"

"I do."

"He must be really proud of you."

She squinted. "I'm just as proud of him. He's a successful businessman."

The Secretary of Defense stood next to a door with a high security placard. "Here's where all the action is. You're going to find this very interesting."

They entered a room packed with technological instruments and large view screens. At the far end was another glass sealed room with a slanted horizontal control panel and hundreds of knobs, switches and computer monitors at each station. "Gentlemen, please be seated. Welcome to my world. This is the main control room for the OPAD project. OPAD stands for 'Operational Project for Asteroid Deflection'. There are several components that make up the twin satellites; each given the task of intercepting a close proximity collision."

The Secretary of Defense interrupted. "Now keep in mind there are other divisions that are working on long range interception. That's not what OPAD is about. These systems have been developed if all else fails. Like an asteroid that suddenly comes upon us from nowhere."

"Does that kind of thing happen? Or let me rephrase that; when's the last time that happened of any consequence?"

"Not in modern times, Senator. But we have plenty of evidence from the past. I don't have to stress that a large asteroid or comet could extinguish life as we know it."

"Not a pleasant prospect. So, how does your system work?"

Beth paced in front of the console. "It's really a duel system. As I speak we have two large generators in geo-synchronous orbit above Houston. We do have the ability to reposition these generators. Each generator is capable of distributing a powerful laser beam directly onto the surface of an asteroid. In theory, that should allow us to push the asteroid out of harms way."

"In theory it sounds good. But will it work?"

Beth hesitated. "Extensive tests are scheduled to begin next month."

"So we really don't know if it works?"

"Senator Blakely, we have done some preliminary testing with promising results. But this intricate of a system requires thorough testing. And that can only be done in the vacuum of space."

"I'm impressed. We should be able to send Washington a good report that our money has been well spent."

"Thank you, Senator. As I told you before, I have two daughters of my own and one day a system like this may save their lives."

That evening in the Anderson home, Beth and her family sat around the dinner table and enjoyed the kind of stories and laughter that many families repeated all around the world. Though Damian kept asking Beth how her guests reacted to the project, she seemed more interested in her children's school activities.

"Leah, what did Miss Cramble say about your drawing?"

"She liked it, mom."

"She should have. It was really good."

Tawnee scooted peas across the plate with her fork. "Mom, you still haven't said if I can go to the concert yet."

Damian kept his head down and continued eating.

"Well, mom?"

"Ask your father."

He pulled two tickets out of his shirt pocket and Tawnee exploded out of her chair. "Just you and me, baby."

"Can I go to my room? I want to call Maddie."

Leah dropped her fork. "Can I go, too?"

"Okay." Beth then glanced over at her husband. "That was nice thing to do. You haven't been to a concert in a while."

"Yeah, I can't wait. Me and twenty thousand screaming girls."

Beth affectionately tickled her husband's hand. "I think you deserve something special tonight. Have anything in mind?"

He wiggled his eyebrows. "I can think of something."

She nestled up behind him and kissed him on the cheek. "You can have anything you want after a foot rub. I've been running around all day."

"You got it, baby. We'll clean up the kitchen later."

After tucking the kids into bed, brushing their teeth and making love, they collapsed onto the bed. Exhausted, Beth looked forward to a good night's sleep. It was a mild evening and their bedroom window was opened a few inches to enjoy the cricket serenade. By two o'clock in the morning, the house was silent and then a phone ring awoke them both.

"Who can that be", asked Damian?

Beth reached over and picked up the receiver. "Yes?" She sat up rigidly and spoke tensely. "What? You're kidding?"

"What is it?"

She threw off the covers. "I got to go."

"Go? Where?"

To Mission Control."

"At this hour?"

"It's an emergency."

By now Damian was wide awake. "What's going on?"

"They didn't say. Only to come down immediately. You got to take the kids to school."

"No problem. Call me when you know something."

Beth arrived at the Johnson Space Center and the base was already on alert. Everyone appeared uneasy as she drove past the guard gate and was stopped by two military police officers in a jeep. They walked up to her. "You Beth Anderson?"

"Yes."

"Come with us, please? You can leave your vehicle here and we'll take care of it."

"Where are we going?"

"To a meeting at a secured location."

They escorted her to a building and down a hallway where a room with a large conference table had been prepared. Two Air Force generals and several civilians, including the director of NASA joined her. "Hello, Beth. Sit down."

"What's going on here?"

"You'll learn soon enough." The NASA chief then addressed the room's occupants. "I'm Dexter Marford. You all know me. Six hours ago the Chinese military reported a large asteroid on a collision course towards Earth. The size of the object is purported to be five to six miles wide." They all mumbled to each other. "Impact is one hundred per cent."

"A rock that large will destroy the planet."

"That's right, general."

"Not acceptable. What are we going to do?"

The other general interrupted. "How did this go undetected?"

"To that question, we have no idea. To the first question, our options are very limited."

"Let's nuke it."

"If this object were days—months away, that might be a viable choice. Impact may be as soon as four hours. A nuclear device would only scatter it. The results would be the same, if not worse."

Everyone in the room was dead silent. Beth covered her face. "There's nothing we can do. It's over."

"Not necessarily, Beth. Our only hope may be the OPAD system."

"It hasn't even been tested."

"No time for trials. Like it or not, we've already assembled your staff and they're waiting for you. We expect you to have the system up and running in a few hours."

"You're making me responsible for over six billion lives?"

"Who else? There's nobody else. We're wasting time. In a few hours the city of Houston is going to see a huge light in the sky."

Beth hurriedly raced towards the OPAD command center. On the way she called her husband. "Damian, listen carefully."

"What's going on, Beth?"

"Get the girls out of bed, get them dressed and come down to the space center."

"What's wrong?"

"Just do what I say. I can't explain now."

"You're scaring me."

You'd better be scared. Go to gate 6A with that special badge I gave you. Give them your name and the code. They'll take you to a location. I'll come to you."

"Are we under attack?"

"Just get my babies down here!"

"Okay, okay. I'm on it."

The four specialists from Beth's team were seated in the control booth with eyes fixated on her. Tim Gaylord, the expert on power systems and Elaine Toles, the laser specialist, were her two most integral staff members. The other two technicians would monitor all the data. "You all know what we're up against. I can't promise anyone this is going to work, but we have to give it our best. I've been told the survival of our planet depends on us. I realize this is a grave responsibility. But under these circumstances, we have no other choice."

Tim held out his hands. "How the hell are we going to alter the trajectory of such a large asteroid? We haven't even tested our systems."

"It's called on the job training." She rested her palm against a horizontal control panel. "It's not going to be easy. We have very little time to figure it out."

Tim nodded. "Let's fire up these generators." He tapped in a long sequence of numbers on his computer and flicked a line of switches along the console. Nothing happened. He repeated the sequence and there was still no response. "I don't understand, Beth. It should power up."

"Let's kick start it. Overload the circuits. We'll send an electrical charge through the relays."

"That might deplete the reserves."

"And your point? If it doesn't start, we're dead anyway."

"Here goes everything." Just as Beth predicted, the large orbital generators came to life. "Should take a little less than two hours to fully charge."

"How much power did we lose in the overload?"

"I can't tell you exactly. But it's minimal."

"Good." She turned to one of the technicians. "I want you to monitor the asteroid's telemetry at all times. I want to know if it diverts from its course, speeds up or slows down—any deviation." She turned to Elaine. "Those lasers better work."

"They will. We've tested them over and over again."

"I have to go. I'll be back soon. Stay alert." Beth vacated the control room and ran down the hallway until she reached a parallel section of the building. She burst into a small room and both daughters ran up to her excitedly. Damian followed closely behind. "Beth, what's happening? Everybody's so uptight."

She signaled him to leave the room. "All right, kids. Go sit down and wait for mommy and daddy."

They complained, but followed her orders. She joined her husband in the hallway. "Okay, let's have it?"

Beth wiped a tear from the corner of her eye. "In a matter of hours, the Earth is going to be impacted by an asteroid the size of a city."

He fell against the wall. "No."

"That's why I wanted you down here; you and the kids. We need to spend what time we have left as a family."

He grabbed both her arms. "You have to do something."

"OPAD is our only hope. But I have to be honest, it's probably not going to work. It wasn't meant for this kind of situation."

"I thought that's exactly what it was meant for?"

"It's difficult to explain. This asteroid is coming so fast that it would have to be intercepted much further out. But we didn't have that luxury. Now it's up to an unproven, untested system."

"You have to make it work. I'm not ready for the end of the world."

"I'm going to do my best."

"What about our kids?"

"We're not going to tell them anything."

"But what do we say right now?"

"That mommy is doing an important test. Tell them we're going to have fun after this. Tell them anything but the truth."

They went back to the room and their daughters were obviously bored. "What about school? Don't we have to go to school, mom?"

"Not today, Tawnee."

"So what are we supposed to do?"

Damian hugged his oldest daughter. "It's only one day. You got your math test next week. They'll be plenty of time to study."

"But Lisa Zimmerman's been bragging that she's going to beat me."

"Don't worry, you'll smoke her."

Leah held onto her mother's arm. "What am I going to do?"

"Guess what? Your father's planning a trip to Disneyworld."

Both daughters cheered demonstratively. "When, when?"

"I've been thinking about staying a week in one of those resorts."

"With swimming pools?"

Damian glanced at his wife painfully and then looked down at Leah. "Yeah. Swimming pools."

Beth kissed her daughters. "Mommy's got to go, but I'll be back soon. Stay with daddy."

The duel power generators were fully charged in one hour and forty-five minutes. Beth had returned to the conference room and prepared to brief them one last time. The NASA director turned to her. "This better be good."

"We can deploy the lasers right now. That will give us approximately two hours of sustained usage. However, it is my professional opinion that it won't be enough to deflect the asteroid."

The general sat up rigidly. "So we're finished?"

"Not necessary. I just feel under these circumstances that the standard operational specs will not deflect the asteroid at such a close range."

"Then what do you propose?"

"Something risky, but with better odds."

"Let's hear it."

"When we first fired up the generators, they didn't respond. So my technician overloaded the relays and it worked. Theoretically the same should happen if we overload the lasers. It will increase the intensity by at least fifty percent. Of course the downside is that it may prematurely burn out the generators. If that happens, nothing we do will save us."

"You think this is the best way?"

"Tim Gaylord, my generator expert, doesn't agree. He thinks it's too risky. But I believe I'm right."

"How long will they last?"

"Instead of two hours, probably one. But then again, they could blow at any time."

The NASA chief closed his eyes and scratched his head. "What do I do? No time for a consensus. We go with you, Beth. It's your call."

"This is one time we can't play it safe."

"It's a big gamble", the General nervously commented.

"General, I have two beautiful daughters. I want to keep them alive. And this is the correct procedure."

Beth returned to the command booth and Tim begrudgingly accepted her decision. "And if it short circuits in a few minutes?"

"Then we all die."

"I don't like it. Let's hope those lasers work."

Elaine sat patiently at her control monitor. "My lasers will function perfectly."

"Tim, the overload."

He programmed the sequence into the panel. "Overload engaged. I'm monitoring the outflow. I prefer to know when it blows."

Beth turned to Elaine. "Deploy the lasers."

"Asteroid tracking aligned. Initiating the transfer." She nodded. "Power levels have increased by forty-seven percent. Lasers activated and on target."

"Report."

"Adjusting number 2 generator beam by three degrees. System functioning within acceptable tolerances."

"You may have to adjust as we go."

"I'm on it."

"Very well. I'll return shortly."

Beth hurried back to her children, whom she found seated impatiently around a table. She knew they couldn't go outside because the asteroid would be clearly visible. "All right, we're going to a place where you can have some fun."

Tawnee stood up with folded arms. "Finally."

Damian ushered them out the door. "Where we going?"

"Follow me." She led them down several hallways and opened the door to a cavernous room with impressive electronics and control consoles. "You can play with any of this stuff. It's all turned off."

Their eyes grew wide. "Really?"

"Just don't break anything."

Damian gazed at her oddly. "Are you sure?"

"Under the circumstances, I'm sure."

While her daughters pretended they were on a spaceship, Beth brought her husband over to the corner of the room and whispered. "OPAD is operating well. It's just a matter of time until we know if it works or not."

"It better work. I can't accept that our children are going to die."

"At least we'll be together."

"Just last night I thought it was going to be another routine day. Kids off to school. You and me off to work."

"It makes you think how precious time is."

"I just wish you were more optimistic."

She pecked him on the cheek. "Sorry. It's just the scientist in me. I'm trained to have a certain amount of skepticism."

"I hope you're wrong and your system's right."

"I got to go."

"I love you. Please save us."

"God knows I'll try."

Beth walked swiftly back to the command center where Tim was shaking his head negatively. "I don't like this."

"What's wrong?"

The overload. There's a decrease of ten per cent."

"How rapid?"

"It's holding at ten per cent. But it slipped fast."

Beth glanced over at Elaine. "Any change in telemetry?"

"Nothing. But the lasers are working at optimum efficiency."

"Very well." She turned to one of the technicians. "You're watching the path?"

"No change."

Beth slid her tongue around her teeth. "Let's bring the number two laser a few more degrees inward. Try to spin the asteroid."

"That may decrease the efficiency of number one."

"It's worth the risk."

"Adjusting now." She looked over at Beth. "I wouldn't advise any further adjustments. It might negate the cause and effect."

"I don't need a lesson in physics."

Tim threw up his hands. "That's it. I'm losing power and it's not abating. There's nothing I can do."

"Best estimate?"

"Thirty minutes, maybe twenty."

"Elaine, we have that much time for the lasers."

"I don't know. I just don't know."

"Power's falling fast, Beth. I don't think it's going to last much longer."

"Damn! I took a gamble with everyone's lives."

Tim arose and embraced her sympathetically. "Don't beat yourself up. It was a noble effort. You did what you had to do."

"But did I make the right decision?"

"We may never get that answer."

Elaine started reconfiguring the beams. "I'm going to pull these beams within five feet of each other."

"A hail Mary toss?"

"Who knows? A concentrated force while I still have over one hundred per cent power."

"You won't have that for long."

"Time to impact?"

The technician checked his instruments. "About an hour, give or take ten minutes."

"And the generators?"

"Another ten minutes at best."

Beth nodded slowly. "If they fail, we're all fired."

The generators began to fluctuate and Beth sat helplessly on a chair against the back wall. Her team had done its best and any more efforts were probably futile. The asteroid was still tracking on its deadly course and the end seemed inevitable. Beth was about to return to her family when one of the technician's head jerked up.

"What's this? A slight deviation in the asteroid's telemetry."

"How much?"

"Perhaps .063."

"Discernable."

"The generators are about to give out."

Elaine shook her head. "Still not enough deflection to matter."

"One degree, two degrees; it's moving!"

Beth restrained her joy. "Okay, this is encouraging. Elaine, overlap the beams."

"I'm way ahead of you. It's spinning."

"Number 2 generator down fifty per cent. We're losing it."

"Steady."

Both generators overloaded completely and went silent. Beth turned to the technician tracking the asteroid.

He hollered and made a fist. "We did it! It's veering off."

On the other side of Saturn and invisible to all the high tech sensing devices on Earth, visitors in a space craft monitored the action as a fat three fingered hand plunged down on a colorfully lit panel. "That was an incredible defense by the Zalandrians in a last effort to deflect V457. Those that have just joined us, it appears that team Zalandria is going to leave this round of Flinger with a scoreless tie and thus take the championship by over all ratings. Team Gelblaxo almost scored and would have pushed this to another round. There is some time left, but Gelblaxo's options are very limited. Team Zelandria is well aware that V458 is probably on the other side of the system's star and they should be able to defend the proximity line around the planet. There's simply not enough time left for this deception to work. Let's go to my colleague, Spuntza, who is in communication with both team leaders."

"That's right. Things look pretty bleak for Gelblaxo. Already four of the ten Zelandrian vessels have moved to an intercept position." Spluntza then displayed the Gelblaxo team leader on the view screen; a being with a mouth on top of its forehead and three eyes protruding from stems around its neck. "Team Gelblaxo, what can you possibly do when your adversary knows your strategy?"

"They may think they know our strategy."

"Unless you have something planned we don't know about, what can you do?" Spluntza then shifted view screens to another being with twin heads and multiple tongues. "I'm now speaking to the Zelandrian team leader. Here you are, ready to take the Flinger finals. Do you think the Gelblexo may have a last second answer?"

The leader was dismissive. "What can they do? They have a rock hidden on the other side of the star and we know it."

"Well, there you have it."

"Thank you, Spluntza, for your insightful commentary. And now it's up to the Gelblaxo. Their ships are getting into position and just as we suspected, Gelblaxo is retrieving V458 now presumably positioned on the other side of the star. Zelandria is countering and there is no chance for success. Wait. It appears that one of the Gelblaxo vessels is having some kind of difficulty. It's heading back to the docking platform. What's this? The Gelblaxo vessel is streaking towards the single moon near the target planet. It's not damaged at all. It's retrieving a smaller rock it must have hidden behind the moon during the confusion of round three. The Zelandrians are adjusting and heading at full speed to intercept. The Gelblaxo vessel has released the rock towards the proximity line. It appears that the Zelandrians will be unable to stop it. This could be one of the most incredible Flinger endings of all time. And yes, they scored! They scored! Unbelievable. A last second victory. The Gelblaxo have now forced another round of Flinger in the Larian system."

In the excitement and jubilation, the announcers, their vessels, support team and contestants zipped out of the solar system in a flash and returned to their home bases. Unfortunately no one retrieved the asteroid from its collision course towards Earth. If it weren't for the quick reactions of one of the cleanup crew vessels, the asteroid would have probably destroyed all life on the planet and would have required some minor sanctions on the league. In the immortal words of a former Flinger commentator: "Oh well, these things happen."

PROJECT

The ten year old boy shivered in the morning frost beneath an overhanging ledge of rock and dirt. He had been on a camping trip with his family and was missing for two days. The search parties had been well organized, but failed to locate him. Helicopters, dogs and all terrain vehicles participated in the hunt, desperately trying to find him before he experienced hypothermia.

Even as the day's sun began to warm is face, his fingertips and toes were almost frozen. The lack of food and water also depleted his energy and without the will to survive, he had all but given up hope. And then he heard a distinct, "hello, hello", above his head. He was about to respond and then he heard another, "hello."

"I'm down here!"

A young boy near his age in a plaid shirt and red cap stuck his head over the ledge and gestured to him with a whirling finger. "Go around and come up to me."

He followed the instructions and was given a helping hand up to a well defined animal trail. "I'm lost."

"Everybody's been looking for you."

"I'm so hungry."

The boy handed him a canteen and a protein bar and pointed down the animal trail. "Your camp's not that far from here. Just keep walking that way and around that big hill. They'll find you."

He drank sloppily from the canteen. "Are you sure? Are you sure?"

"Just follow the trail." The boy in the cap then started walking in the opposite direction.

"Where are you going?"

He didn't turn around.

Back at the campsite a television reporter stood in front of her camera operator as others behind them erratically dashed from one tent to the other. "Its day two and there's still no sign of Gerald Sanders. They've expanded their search, but nobody's had a sighting. Gerald's parents have been up here the whole time and they are understandably very upset. Their son was lost on a hike and hasn't been seen since. Fortunately the temperatures have not been that cold, but that's going to change soon."

On the other side of the camp there seem to be some kind of commotion. The newscaster was distracted and signaled to the camera operator that they should move towards an area where euphoric celebrations were taking place. The reason was clear when the newscaster recognized the Sanders boy. She quickly straightened her hair and composed herself. "This is a miracle. I'm thrilled to report that Gerald Sanders has just returned after missing for two days. His parents are hugging him and everyone around here is just elated. Again, missing boy Gerald Sanders is alive and well."

That afternoon in his hospital bed, Gerald repeated his account to several news agencies. He recalled the unknown boy with the red cap that had found him. He had no other details, nor any idea of where his young rescuer had come from. The authorities made some inquiries about any missing children in the area, but when none materialized they closed the case. For the media, the story about the unknown rescuer would be just another curiosity for a few days' news cycle.

On the other side of the country in a small town in Maine, a twelve year old girl had been missing for three days. She was last seen walking home from school and never made it home. Her frantic parents immediately contacted the police who then interviewed those that had last seen her. It soon became a national story as police checked house to house and the entire town searched the nearby woods.

Cindy Morrow went in and out of consciousness for her lack of sleep. Her mouth was taped and she was restrained by steel bracelets around her wrists and ankles in a dark room inside a basement. With only a crack of light shining under a single door, she awaited the middle aged man who had abducted her for purposes she could only imagine. He gave her food and drink and she begged him to free her, but he responded with a sinister laugh.

Hours later the door opened up again. She squinted from the brightness and beheld a young boy standing in front of her. "Are you Cindy Morrow?"

"Yes I am. Please help me."

He put his finger over his lips to quiet her. "Don't say anything. He's coming. I'll get you out. I promise." He closed the door, hid behind the stairs and waited for the man to approach her. The boy then lifted a ceramic pot over his head and smashed it down on the man's skull, knocking him unconscious. He then opened the door and when she saw it was the boy, she cried out joyfully. He smiled at her. "Now you just wait here. I'll go get somebody to help you out of those chains."

"No, don't leave me!"

"Don't worry, you're all right now."

In a New York City television studio, the anchor reported breaking news. "Good evening, we begin tonight with an amazing development in the state of Maine. Cindy Morrow, a twelve year old missing girl, has been found in the basement of Alfred Kepple, a neighbor six blocks away from her house. The police had been canvassing the area, but failed to turn up anything. Oddly enough Cindy claimed she was rescued by an unknown young boy. The police claim they received a call and were directed to Kepple's home. What makes this story especially intriguing is the similarity with another rescue that took place in the mountains on a camping trip. In both incidences, a young unidentified male saved their lives. However, the descriptions of the rescuers were vastly different. Again, missing girl Cindy Morrow has been found alive and unharmed in a neighbor's basement."

On a Minnesota highway, a young mother and her six month old baby girl traveled through a mountain pass on a cold, snow free night. Her daughter was sound asleep in the car seat while her mother sang along to a country music station. There were a few other cars on the road and she was driving at a safe speed. When a deer unexpectedly jumped in front of the automobile, she swerved, lost control, slid off the side of the road and slammed into a tree. The mother was killed instantly and the child suffered a gash in her head from a piece of loose jagged metal.

Ten miles away was a hospital. The duty nurse couldn't believe her eyes when a boy walked inside holding a wrapped up baby with serious injuries. The child was rushed to the emergency ward where the doctor's attended her. When the nurse returned to get information from the boy, he was no where to be found. The sheriff had later located the mother's vehicle and to the surprise of everyone, the story was very similar to other accounts about a young guardian angel rescuing endangered children.

Shortly after the Minnesota car accident, a children's clinic with an excellent reputation for curing young cancer patients treated a boy named Kyle in the last stages of his illness. To the average citizen, these kinds of places were sad and dreary; but this particular clinic was well known for its caring staff, upbeat attitudes and advanced techniques. Like many cutting edge facilities, the doctors and nurses kept the children in high spirits with fun and games.

The doctors were now preparing Kyle's mother and father for the devastating results when a series of treatments fail. Mr. and Mrs. Austin stood at their son's bed side as Kyle was examined by his personal physician, who gestured for them to leave the room.

"I've just looked over Kyle's most recent tests and I'm afraid the results do not look promising."

Mrs. Austin's could barely keep her head up. "Please. Do something."

"I'm sorry. There is little more I can do."

She whimpered. "But the results were promising."

Mr. Austin held onto his wife. "Are you sure, doctor?"

"When we perform these procedures we look for some improvement. I'll admit that at first there were some encouraging signs. But over the last three tests, Kyle's health has degraded. Your son is not responding to the treatments. Further treatment may just make him sicker than he already is."

"So there's no hope?"

"Mr. and Mrs. Austin, I'm going to level with you. At some point in any patient's regiment, there comes a time when we can do more damage than good. We've come to that point. If this were my child, I would allow nature to take its course."

Mrs. Austin tried to hold back her tears. "How can we do that?"

"The drugs are doing him more harm. Let Kyle enjoy what's left of his life."

"How Long", asked Mr. Austin in an emotionless daze?

"Kyle's been fighting this for three years. I'm reluctant to put a time on it. I still am a believer in miracles."

"How long, Doctor?"

"Three months, perhaps a little more."

"Thank you. We needed to know."

They returned to the room and found it difficult to smile at their son, who was always smiling at them.

Kyle liked his night nurse, who read him stories and brought him occasional treats. Eventually he fell asleep and the nurse dimmed the lights. He slept for a few hours and then something woke him up. At his bed side was a pale young boy about his age. Kyle didn't think he was a patient because he was wearing blue jeans and a plaid shirt.

"Who are you?"

"My name is Eddie."

"Hi, Eddie. Why are you here?"

"Your name is Kyle, right?"

"Yes, but visiting hours are over."

He confidently grinned. "Not for us. You're very sick, aren't you?"

"I'm going to die."

"You're not going to die. I won't let that happen."

"There's nothing you can do, Eddie."

He reached out and touched Kyle's arm. Nothing happened at first, and then Eddie's eyes fluttered and body trembled. Kyle immediately called for his nurse. When she arrived in his room, she saw the young boy passed out on the floor.

"You have to help him."

She took his pulse. "Who is he?"

"Eddie. He said his name was Eddie."

The nurse immediately called a code blue emergency and within minutes a doctor and two other nurses responded with medical equipment and a gurney. They lifted the boy onto the gurney and a doctor worked quickly to ascertain his condition. They took him to the ICU, performed a CT scan and then drew blood for analysis. "Who is this child and where did he come from?"

"I don't know, Doctor. He was in Kyle Austin's room."

"And you're certain he's not a patient?"

"I've checked all the files and we can't identify him."

The Doctor continued the examination. "He's in a coma. Let's notify the police and see if they have a missing child."

The nurse noticed that Kyle was standing near the doorway. "What are you doing here, sweetheart?"

"Making sure Eddie's okay."

"Let's get you back to bed."

"Is he going to be all right?"

"We don't know yet. But you have to get back to your room."

Kyle waved his arms around and exuberantly jumped up and down. "Why? I'm feeling great."

She finally recognized that he was vigorously animated. "How can that be?"

"I'm telling you that I feel the way I was before I got sick."

She leaned over and grabbed onto his arms. "You do look different. You look really well. How's that possible?"

"I'm not sick anymore. Eddie cured me."

She stood up with her mouth wide open. "How could he do that?"

"I don't know. But I'm really hungry. Can I have a sandwich?"

"But you'll throw up."

"No, I won't. I'm really hungry. I can eat." He squeezed her hand with a renewed strength he had not demonstrated for many years. "Let's go. I want to eat something." He ran ahead of her down the hallway. She could barely keep up.

The doctors had given the police officers a report of Eddie's unexplainable appearance and illness. When they examined the tests it was clear that Eddie was suffering from the same blood disease that had overtaken Kyle. It wasn't until the next day when they had examined Kyle, they realized a miracle had occurred. Against all scientific and medical odds, Kyle was in spontaneous remission of his cancer. With the exception of some residual cell readings, Kyle had been essentially cured.

When Mr. and Mrs. Austin visited the clinic, they were overjoyed when they saw their son playing with children in their first stages of illness. Kyle was as enthusiastic and rambunctious as he had been prior to his cancer. Still perplexed, the doctors couldn't explain the miraculous cure. "Mr. and Mrs. Austin, I don't know what to say. There is no medical explanation for this. But your son is going to live a long time."

"This is fantastic!"

"It was nothing we did."

Kyle ran up to his parents and leaped into his father's arms. "Isn't it great? And I owe it all to Eddie."

"Who?"

The doctor's eyes wandered. "Eddie. This young boy that we found in Kyle's room. He's still in a coma."

"Who is he?"

"We don't know. He doesn't seem to have any family and the police have no idea who he is."

"Eddie cured me. He touched me and I was better."

"We'd like to keep Kyle under observation for about a week. Make certain that he's truly in remission. But my guess is that he'll be coming home very soon."

"I don't know what to say. This is a prayer answered."

In the ICU unit, Eddie's eyelids began to quiver and his fingers wiggled. He slowly regained his vision while the staff hovered over him. "Hello, Eddie. You're name is Eddie, right? How are you feeling?"

"Not so good."

"Where are you from?"

He was confused. "I don't know. I only know my name."

"Do you have a father or mother?"

"I only know my name is Eddie." He lifted his arms and realized he was connected to intravenous lines. "Where am I?"

"A hospital."

"That boy, Kyle. How is he?"

"You remember Kyle? He's doing just fine. He said you cured him."

"I think I did cure him."

"Can you tell me how?"

His eyes blinked rapidly and then he vomited. "I feel sick."

"We're going to give you something to settle your stomach. You can sleep now."

A police officer met with Eddie's inquisitive doctor. "Did you find anything about my young patient?"

"Nothing, so far. No missing child alerts. The orphanages haven't reported any missing children from there either."

"Thank you, officer. Keep trying."

"Can I speak to him?"

"He's very ill. He's sleeping now. Perhaps another time."

The following day Eddie was fully conscious and had been interviewed by the police. The doctor's recommended that Eddie was well enough to leave the ICU and moved him to another ward where he could interact with other children. Eddie was likable and soon endeared himself to the patients and staff. As expected he drew media attention when the networks reported his story in the hopes of finding out his true identity.

A nurse was doing her rounds when Eddie tugged on her uniform. "Oh, hello Eddie. What can I do for you?"

"I need to see Leann Wheeler."

"She's very ill with brain cancer."

"Please let me see her."

She hesitated. "All right. But only for a minute."

The nurse brought Eddie to the ward housing the sickest children. Leann was only nine years old and could hardly lift her bandaged head. Eddie walked over to her and touched her forearm. Within seconds, the nurse was stunned when she smiled effervescently and sat up in bed. And then Eddie's eyes turned up into his sockets and he passed out on the floor.

They rushed him to the ICU where it was determined that he was in a coma. The nurse that had witnessed Leann Wheeler's miraculous recovery brought her to the doctor, who couldn't believe his eyes. "Leann?"

"Eddie cured me."

He glanced with amazement at the nurse. "How is this possible?"

"I have no explanation. Eddie asked to see her and then touched her arm. She was healed immediately. It was a miracle."

"This Eddie is a very special child." The doctor's phone rang. He answered it, nodded a few times and then lowered his head. "That was the lab on Eddie's latest results. He now has brain cancer."

The nurse smiled at Leann. "He took her cancer. Just like that Austin kid."

The doctor arranged a news conference and relayed to the public that Eddie had been responsible for the miraculous cures of two children. He was asked several questions; including those from reporters that suggested similarities to a young boy saved in the forest, a kidnapped girl in Maine and a baby in Minnesota. Although the police had discounted these as coincidences because the physical descriptions varied, many in the country believed that a real guardian angel was responsible.

Eddie, who had regained consciousness, was barely alive and struggled to communicate.

"How are you?"

"I'm tired."

The doctor massaged his forehead. "You've a very brave young boy. Many have said that you are an angel."

"Why?"

"You don't know? You cured those children. You're famous now."

"I don't want to be famous. I just wanted to help. I wish I felt better to help more of them."

"You've done enough."

"I'm going to die soon."

"Yes, you are."

"That's okay."

"Eddie, are you sure you don't know who your family is?"

He inhaled his last breath. The doctor, who had seen so much agony and despair, wept uncontrollably. Later on he faced the media and reported that Eddie had succumbed to his illness. Eddie's body was taken to the morgue, where it laid under a sheet. And then something very unusual happened. Eddie stood silently in the middle of the room and was transformed from a human being to an alien with an elongated head, large eyes, no ears, thin arms and ten fingered hands. A light came upon him and he was whisked aboard a star vessel where he was greeted by two others of his kind.

"Mother, father . . ."

"Welcome, son. Did you accomplish your assignment?"

"It was exactly what I had hoped for. I can't wait for school to begin."

"Your mother and I are very proud of you. If we're done here, we will leave this sector."

"I'm ready."

The vessel disappeared from high above earth and they sped towards their home planet. The first day of school began as his classmates gathered in the multileveled auditorium for a special awards ceremony. The teacher stepped up to the podium and rested her twenty fingers over the edges of the flat surface. "We're here to honor the winner of this year's project." There was a steady applause. "As you know, every year students are assigned a project to visit another world and report the impact they had upon it. In past years, most students have selected civilizations under the status of Pre-Contact Recognition. This year a young student named Tef Pacor selected a planet that is not expected to attain that status for many years to come. His bold approach has not only won him this year's competition, but the right to ask for special status for this planet from the Division Hierarchy for an early upgrade." She stepped away from the podium. "So it is my pleasure to introduce the winner of this year's project competition, Tef Pacor."

Tef's proud parents embraced him before he made his way up to the podium. When the applause died down, he began to address the assembly. "Thank you. I am honored. I chose a planet called earth. I knew they had a barbaric reputation and many of those facts were true. But when I researched their world, I did find some positive attributes. They were mostly peaceful and with some help may eventually become an accepted member of the galaxy. I wanted to study the reaction of these people to acts of kindness. I chose subjects equivalent to my age that were in life threatening situations. I found that these people really cared about each other. So I ask that other students would evaluate worlds like these in the future and not be reluctant to help them out. Thank you for this award and I'm sure we're all looking forward to another productive year at school."